Elizabeth Sisson

Gathered thistles

A story of two households

Elizabeth Sisson

Gathered thistles
A story of two households

ISBN/EAN: 9783337150648

Printed in Europe, USA, Canada, Australia, Japan

Cover: Foto ©Andreas Hilbeck / pixelio.de

More available books at **www.hansebooks.com**

GATHERED THISTLES

OR A

STORY OF TWO HOUSEHOLDS

BY

S. ELIZABETH SISSON

1897
HAMMOND BROTHERS
FREMONT, NEB.

TO MY HUSBAND: Without whose kindly co-operation and larger faith this little "home story" had not ventured from the quiet of a parsonage closet shelf, this book is lovingly dedicated.   S. E. S.

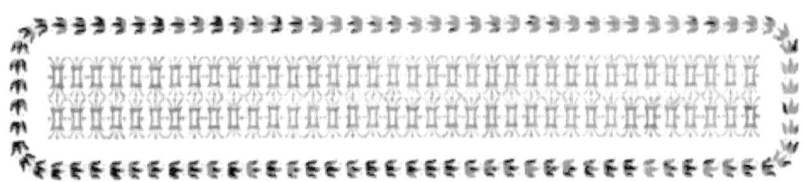

TABLE OF CONTENTS.

CHAPTER VIII.

CHAPTER IX.

CHAPTER X.

CHAPTER XI.

CHAPTER XII.

CHAPTER XIII.

CHAPTER XIV.

CHAPTER XV.

CHAPTER XVI.

CHAPTER XVII.

CHAPTER XVIII.

CHAPTER XIX.

CHAPTER XX.

CHAPTER XXI.

CHAPTER XXII.

CHAPTER XXIII.

CHAPTER XXIV.

CHAPTER XXV.

CHAPTER I.

A DOUBLE WEDDING.

THE TIME was away back in the forties, and the morning was one of the balmiest in blossom-crowned May when Lynton, a little New England village, was strangely astir.

It was easy to see, upon ever so slight an investigation, that this unusual activity centered in the rustic, ivy-covered village church, for the sound of merry young voices from within was borne out upon the fragrant air, through the doors which stood invitingly open. A glance through them shows a group of the village young people who with evergreens and flowers are making the plain, almost stern walls of the room radiant with beauty.

This in preparation for a much anticipated event, a double wedding. As the wedding hour is rapidly nearing it may be well to have an introductory word concerning not only the happy couples who are to be the principals in the event, but the quaint little village of Lynton as well. Picturesque Lynton, its friends lovingly call it.

The latter was situated, as has already been said, in one of the New England states; a portion of it appeared to half cling or **perch upon** the rocky hill upon which it was built, the remainder **stretched on across** Hazel Run, a tiny **stream, losing itself in the** fertile meadow beyond, **the only bit of land really** suitable for tillage.

In a brown, weather-beaten cottage **in the hill** clinging part, lived Rachel Ewing, with her father and mother, she being the oldest of a large family.

There is a bit of yard in front of the cottage, scrupulously clean, while a rocky walk, bordered **on either** side by beds of springing crocuses and gorgeous Easter flowers leads up **to** the open door, through which, on this same May morning, the breezes come in unhindered.

How tidy and home-like is the little front room, though the furnishings are very plain. A bright rag carpet is upon the floor. There are some comfortable looking wooden chairs, and in one corner a stand, upon which we notice a substantially bound family Bible, a book of Psalms set to music, and a few other volumes, **mostly of** the sterner religious kind of the day, for Jacob **Ewing was a** God-fearing man. Daily had his children seen him take down the Bible and heard him read, with an awesome voice, lessons for **their** guidance.

At the rear of the house stood a great apple **tree** under whose spreading branches, during many a **happy** hour, **the** children of the home had found a delightful play ground. This to-day had yielded a part of its treasures for the room's adornment.

On either side of the ancient clock, which stood in the exact center of a very tall wood mantel, was a bowl of fragrant apple blossoms, while in a little room just back of the one that has engrossed our attention, deft fingers are pinning sprays of the same sweet blossoms at the throat, and twining others in the hair of fair young Rachel, one of the brides for whom evergreens and flowers are gracing the village church.

The stiff, yet relentlessly true finger of the old family clock points the hour at which the walk to the church shall begin, and John Stevenson walks in to claim his bride.

Amid the hurry, yes, and heartaches, of this supreme moment, we turn and speed down the rocky street, and on across the little wooden bridge. Here the houses are seen—perhaps not cleaner nor yet more homelike than in the hilly part, but a more liberal use of paint,—shutters at the windows, and here and there a pretentious two-story, tells of greater worldly prosperity.

At the gateway leading up to one of the most comfortable of these homes stands an old family carryall, and just now, out from her mother's doorway (her father having lain in the church yard more than a year) Margaret Allen is coming, leaning upon the arm of William Newton, whose name she is so soon to bear.

Now while the two bridal parties are on the way to the church, there will be time for a hasty glance at the home of Margaret, and to glean something of the history of the two girls.

From the days when Rachel Ewing and Margaret Allen first trudged off together to the village school, a peculiar friendship had existed between the two. Though Margaret's father had owned much of the fertile meadow land beyond the village, while Rachel's could claim as his own but the weather-beaten cot that housed his bairns, yet so sturdy and common-sense was the New England atmosphere of that day, that because of the honesty of purpose and integrity of heart which Jacob Ewing was known to possess, he stood quite as high in the esteem of his neighbors as though broad acres had been his; hence there had not been a thought of anything incongruous in the abiding friendship between the girls.

Together they had sat at the low, wooden desks of the school; later on their voices had rung out together in song in the church in whose communion each had been raised. It was fitting, therefore, that to-day they should stand together at its simple chancel while the mystic words were said that should change them, at a bound, from light-hearted girls into women, looking fearlessly into the face of the future.

Great interest had centered in this event, for not only were the young couples well known, but

it was further known, that on the morning following the marriage they were to leave forever
their village home, make the long journey westward, and that somewhere on those western
prairies, of whose wildness, rumor had much to
say, two new homes would arise. The two great
covered wagons that were to bear them westward
had stood for the last week back of the village
smithy, objects of supreme interest; hence it was
not strange that at an early hour the church had
been filled, with an eager assemblage of friends.
After this digression, we too will join the waiting
assembly, and it will not be out of place if, as the
wedded pairs slowly pass down the aisles, we turn
with the audience for a passing glance.

John Stevenson and his bride Rachel are in
front. There is no mistaking the plain, rugged
honesty of his face, while the browned hands,
indeed the whole bearing, in some subtle manner
tells of a life experience that has been largely a
hand-to-hand struggle with a rocky New England
farm.

Unconsciously though, there is that in the face
which speaks of a victory gained. The eyes rest
lovingly upon his bride with an air of fond, trust-
ful proprietorship.

Large of build, rugged, kindly of disposition, the
student of human nature sees at once that he will
lean upon his wife, consult with her, be influenced
by her as neither she nor he suspects. Thus far,

life has held **but** few joys for him, for his mother had died many years ago, and with her all that might have made his life joyous. **No wonder that** he invites the future.

And she? Beautiful? Well, they **who know her best** scarcely think of beauty, yet there is no plainness **in** the clear complexion, nor in the shapely hands, though these are hard with toil; but **not** one in all that company of village folk is **thinking** of these, but rather of the loving, helpful **spirit** which shines in the large gray—at times almost blue—eyes. **As she is passing,** these accidentally rest **for a moment upon the eager up**-turned face of a neighbor's child, and **in an instant** the little heart is gladdened by a smile of recognition and in the smile, and the self-forgetfulness that allowed it, is mutely revealed—that innate, **nameless** "something"—which causes dumb **animals to** instinctively turn **to** its possessor for protection, **and little** children **to** bring their childish trials.

Though a smile so readily comes **to the** mouth, **there is a firmness about the** clearly cut lips; yes, **a** firmness that **it** is easy to believe might become **akin** to sternness. Somehow as Rachel passes out the rustic church we involuntarily recall grewsome stories of young girl martyrs, and we mentally aver, this New England girl-wife will have abiding principles and maintain them.

If John Stevenson and his bride **have proven** an interesting study, William Newton and his fair

Margaret are not less so. The former had come to Lynton but a twelve-month ago as the manager of a large saw mill, which was fast changing the great forests about Lynton into acres of stumps, which later should give way to waving fields of ripening grain.

So well had he deported himself that he not only became a strong factor in the village life, winning the esteem of all, and the love of beautiful Margaret Allen as well. It is easy to see that nature has cast him in an entirely different mold from that of rugged John Stevenson. There is a restless acuteness about the eyes which indicate greater business ability. There is about him an easy air in his smart new wedding suit, and a something which proclaims an acquaintance with the world.

He is a communicant at the altars of the same church as are the others, but seeing him we can but speculate as to what would be his course should duty and worldly prosperity clash.

But John Stevenson's eyes do not rest more lovingly upon his bride's than do William Newton's upon the fair Margaret; however different otherwise they may be, they are one in love for their chosen companions.

As has been said, Margaret's home had been one of comfort and plenty. Her parents were found each Sabbath among the worshipers, yet to serve God had not been with Richard Allen, as with Jacob Ewing, the supreme motive of life.

Much dearer to him than thoughts of God had
been his fertile acres with accompanying flocks
and herds. Indeed in his heart he had fixed for
himself a creed, the liberality of which, had they
but known it, would have startled the staid people
he worshiped with. Yet his family understood it
well, and none better than Margaret. From the
time she could toddle she had been his chosen
companion.

As she grew older, various traits peculiar to the
father appeared in the child, until it came to be a
saying with the other members of the family,
"Margaret is father over again."

We have already said she was beautiful. As
she left the altar on her wedding day she looked
the embodiment of loveliness. Added to rare regularity of features, were a beautiful form, graceful
carriage, and an almost faultless complexion. A
wavy mass of brown hair was brushed back from
the forehead and coiled about the shapely head.
Seeing her we see a beautiful picture; yet, as with
many another picture, there is a sense of dissatisfaction. Can it be that in the graceful curl of
those lips, in the poise of that delicate chin, there
is a hint of selfishness? Or do the eyes, dark hazel
as they are, lack in gentleness? We can scarcely
tell. Yet the face is not one we would care to go
to with a heartache, especially if to ease the ache
self-denial would be required.

Just now she is strong in the new love which has

stirred her heart, and she is bravely going to the hardships of pioneer life. Indeed if there are any hardships, they are lost in the strong glamour which love and distance have thrown about that strange new life beyond.

But the last echo has died out from the church and each couple are now in separate homes. Many tears mingle with the wedding festivities, for the covered wagons stand now, one at Rachel's and one at Margaret's door, and with an agony the young people cannot suspect, each mother packs away in the roomy rear such articles as space will permit. There are chests of linens, of bedding, jars of home-made sweets, and provisions for the long journey.

The next day, amid sobs and heartaches, the home nest is forever left. Groups of villagers gather at the brow of the hill from whence the road stretches on westward. They look long and earnestly, and finally turn each to their homes. They have seen disappear around the curve the last faint flutter of white. The village home of Rachel and Margaret would know them no more.

The old, yet ever new miracle had been re-enacted. The stranger of yesterday becomes more than home, parents, or friends. Strange? No, for centuries before He foreshadowed this home-leaving when he said: "They twain shall become one flesh."

CHAPTER II.

HOWEVER great the sympathy that might bid us linger with those in the broken homes, our interest henceforth lies with those just out of sight, and to them we turn.

Slowly the great wagons creaked on. Margaret in the agony of the parting had flung herself upon an improvised couch which loving hands had provided for her comfort, and lay there bitterly sobbing. Rachel, with tear-stained face, kept fluttering a bit of white cambric as a last adieu, until a bend in the road shut out forever the little village. Presently the last familiar hill or farmhouse was passed; new roadside scenes claimed the attention, and it began to dawn upon those brave young people that the old life was gone. Yet a future, fascinating in its very strangeness, awaited them.

One of the happiest qualities of youth is its elasticity. A wave of sorrow may sweep over it before which it bows as a sapling before a storm, but such is its natural spring that it speedily rights itself, and is erect again. So our young friends soon found much to interest them in this novel experience.

There were meals to be cooked by the wayside. The woods abounded in game; squirrels leaped among the branches of the trees and chattered noisily down. There were great flocks of quail and of wild turkeys. More than once as they came to ford a stream they would startle a herd of timid deer. There was a brace of trusty rifles in each wagon, so the meals were always supplied with the choicest meats. Then there was the novelty of going to sleep with the stars blinking down so familiarly.

As has been said, the journey began in May. Many of the streams were still swollen from the spring rains, and were without bridges. The roads, in some places not more than a bridle path, were at times almost impassable. The plan was to reach Pittsburgh, there embark upon flatboats and journey down the Ohio River as far as Cincinnati, already a prosperous city. Once there, they expected to make the remainder of the journey in their wagons over the National Road, this being a kind of pike or "built road," under national supervision (as its name indicates), which before the era of railroads contributed in no small measure to the rapid settlement of the states as far west as Indiana.

Wonderful stories of the rich prairies that formed so large a part of that great western country known as Illinois had reached their eastern home. These

marvelous tales of the soil's fertility as well as the
unusual business facilities, had made this their ob-
jective point.

So they jolted along, day after day, on this
strange bridal journey.

The modern young husband buys a ticket, and
he and his bride whirl rapidly away. They "do"
mountain or seaside resort, or "tip" waiters in
European hotels, return at length to their homes,
weary, already disgusted with life—happily if not
with each other.

Our old fashioned lovers proceeded more slowly.
What if now and then the road *was* rough, or there
was an hour's excitement over a swollen stream, or,
as happened one night, a great bear should poke
his nose into the rear of one of the wagons. The
greater part of the time the skies were blue. Birds
in all the ecstacy of home-building sang them their
most joyous songs, and they had—each other. And
what with plans for the homes that were to be, the
days were none too long; and Pittsburgh was at
length reached.

Good weather attended the travelers in their
float down the Ohio. The flatboats in which
they journeyed were constructed with a kind of
sheltered room (cabin) for the travelers, and an
enclosed outer deck for wagons and horses. Black
Nell, one of the horses John had driven, rebelled at
this new experience, and caused quite a commotion

one night by an attempt to jump overboard, but at length became reconciled to the inevitable.

Perhaps in all Rachel's life she had not known so much leisure, and it was to her a never ceasing delight to watch the green shadowy outlines of the shore.

At Cincinnati they disembarked, and certainly the world was going West, for there were many covered wagons like their own, and in company with some of these they began their journey over the comparatively smooth "National Road."

They might have gone, as did many emigrants of that day, the entire journey down the Ohio and thence up the Mississippi, but the added cost was a barrier; besides, they wanted to judge for themselves of the country, and the best place to locate.

Indianapolis, then a thrifty young city, was reached; still the horses heads were turned westward, and the Wabash valley was reached.

"Oh Dear," said Margaret, one morning after they had resumed their journey:

"What kind of a road is this, why—;" but the sentence was lost, for just then the front wheels of the wagon gave a lurch downward. The horses gave a sudden pull or Margaret would certainly have been thrown to the ground. These plunges and jerks amid the slushiest and stickiest mud the travelers had ever known, continued throughout the day, causing more discomfort than they had yet known. The smooth National Road having ended, they were experiencing a stretch of "corduroy road," which for the benefit of the modern bicycler on asphalt it may be explained, was made by cutting lengths from trees of various sizes and laying them crosswise in the slush or mud. As these lengths vary in size from saplings to respectable trees the jolting can be imagined. It was little wonder that Margaret exclaimed in agony, nor that all rejoiced when, after a weary length, the smart young city of Springfield, Illinois was reached, where they had decided to stop for a short period of rest, or until they could fix upon a permanent location.

Among the travelers they had fallen in with during their journey were several who were loud in their praises of the wonderful advantages held out to settlers by Burton, a mere stripling of a town on the Illinois River. These agreed that this must shortly become a manufacturing center, citing as arguments its superior water power and the enterprise of its citizens, manifested already by the building of a railroad connecting it with the growing interior towns of the State, and promising to push on farther westward.

As both Rachel and Margaret needed rest, it was decided that they should remain where they were, and their husbands should join a party of men who would visit Burton and other points if necessary.

Once there, it did not take the keen business eye of William Newton long to discover the advantages of the young town. Moreover, a chance of steady employment offered. Upon the banks of the river stood a newly completed flouring mill, which being the only one in all that section would be kept busy grinding meal and flour. By a happy chance he secured a position not greatly inferior to that of manager, and so considered himself fortunate.

The rich, black soil of the gently undulating prairies that crept up to the river's edge, and upon which the town was built, charmed John Stevenson, used as he had been to the rocky hills about Lynton, and he counted himself fortunate when he had bargained for one hundred and sixty acres not two miles from the town. Fortunate, though years of hard work, and, as farmers phrase it, of good luck, must be his portion, before he could call those acres his own; fortunate, though upon the land there was not a roof to shelter either man or beast.

The question of homes being settled they lost no time in joining the waiting ones at Springfield.

Perhaps it has been hardly fair, in that we have left these young girls alone so long, yet they have not been unhappy. They had each grown so weary of the last one hundred miles that they welcomed the rest of their quiet lodging house. Besides, if they cared to go out there was much to interest them in the strange new western life.

Their curiosity and interest was greatly aroused by what they heard concerning a "gathering," in the neighborhood; new to them, but certainly from the conversation a feature of the new life. It was called a *Camp*-meeting, as they learned, because many would come, either from a distance or from the neighborhood, camp out, and spend the time in religious service, but such strange stories as were told, not only of the services but of the minister in charge—indeed, his original sayings were a fruitful theme among the lodgers at every meal.

"Well, one thing sure," both Rachel and Margaret agreed, "We will visit the grounds and see for ourselves before we go further."

To this, their husbands upon their return readily assented, and the next day set out to attend an evening service.

The camp ground, as the place of meeting was called, was simply a piece of woods in which an attempt had been made to clear out the underbrush. As the party drove into the deep shade of the woods, a weird scene presented itself. Great flaring tallow dips nailed here and there to the trees lent an uncanny air to the whole.

The tenters had for shelter the rudest kind of board tents; indeed such were fortunate, the majority sleeping under their wagons.

The platform upon which the preacher stood had been made by felling two trees of about the same size, cutting away the tops, and nailing upon the larger ends a floor of unplaned boards.

But the preaching: "Surely there had never before been heard any so forceful, or so peculiar in

its immediate effects." So, at any rate, thought
our little group of New Englanders.

Pathos, sublimity, caustic wit, scathing rebuke of
sin, of sinners, even of individuals, jostled each
other from the speaker's lips, who was none other
than Peter Cartwright, one of the most unique per-
sonalities of the Illinois of that day. Tall, and of
rugged build, with hair brushed back in a kind of
shock from his forehead, he towered a very giant
come to announce the destruction of the wicked.
His eyes seemed to flash fire, especially when a
miscalculating band of rowdies thought to intimi-
date the preacher and the congregation. Rachel
had heard sermons all her life, but for personal
directness nothing to equal this. The preacher
taught and urged a distinct work of grace in the
heart and a consecration of one's life, whatever be
their calling, to the Lord.

The sermon was followed by the altar service,
and such a service! How they crowded the rude
wooden bench, young and old. Presently a sister
"got" religion. " Look, look at her face!" Rachel
excitedly pulled the sleeve of John for him to see.
It seemed actually transformed, for the woman was
plain in appearance and evidently a daughter of
toil. " Hear her shout!" Now another takes up
the strain. Back in the audience a little knot has
gathered about a prostrate form. It is that of a
man who has been "seeking" for several days. He
lies rigid, motionless, to all appearances dead. The

friends, nothing alarmed, sing and pray and wait
for him to "come through," which he does after a
time, with shouts of joy.

Strange, blessed history of the pioneer church.
The so-called refinement of a later day may smile,
and with delicately pursed lips may whisper "eccentricities!" but after all it is borne in upon us, that
these fathers and mothers "got" a something that
lifted them above the hardships of a frontier life, a
something that in many instances transformed the
wickedest into the most devout, something that implanted that farseeing self-denial which founded the
colleges and built the churches that together have
made to-day's boasted civilization possible. In
short, they "came through" to such a high type of
Christian life that we may well withhold our criti-
cism and be proud to do them homage.

When John and Rachel Stevenson found themselves alone, that night, there was a quiet talk
between them—and as a result of the evening's
strange service, a consecration of their lives in
a sense different from any they had ever
known took place. In another room William and
Margaret too discussed what they had seen and
heard, but with them the grotesque and eccentric
held chief place.

The hospitality and welcome accorded to strangers was a strong feature of the day, and the little
party made many acquaintances before leaving the
grounds, among whom was Mr. Cartwright himself.

Though his eyes may have flashed as he rebuked an offender, there was no mistaking their kindly spirit as he questioned them concerning their plans. As a father might, he urged the immediate duty of identifying themselves with Christian people, pointing out that the habits formed in the first years would shape the whole life. While talking he drew from the cavernous depths of a pair of saddle bags close at hand, some books and what appeared to be copies of a newspaper. For a moment he paused, while from under the shaggy brows a look at once both keen and critical darted from one to another. He continued "you will want in the new home not only religion as a corner stone, but intelligence, and whether you read, and what you read will come to mean everything; therefore however small your income, I entreat you, spend a part of it for good books. Further, if your homes are to be intelligent in the best sense, you will need a kind of literature that even books do not supply. Here are a few copies of a periodical devoted to the home; indeed it is called *The Christian Home.* Perhaps its reading may not only make the last miles of your journey pleasanter, but show you your need of such a friend." Then telling them that he should see them again, as Burton was one of his preaching points, he bade them God speed.

The following morning the last stage of the journey was resumed. William had much to tell Margaret of the new home and business, and neither

gave a thought to the kindly preacher except to
laugh together at certain eccentricities and oddities
of manner; but in the rear John and Rachel jolted
on, and at times their conversation was as serious
as even the zealous Mr. Cartwright could have
desired.

CHAPTER III.

GETTING SETTLED.

ANOTHER day and night found these emigrants in what was to be their new home, Burton. When each had grown to be old, they never forgot the strange newness, and unfinished appearance of the town. The streets were yet grassy, and such little houses! Nearly all of logs. Still there was an air of bustling activity. People went about as if there was a world to build, and but a little time to build it in, and none caught the contagion quicker than William Newton. He at once began work in the mill, and in a little cottage, conveniently near, Margaret began her housekeeping.

This little home was very plain on the outside, but warm and cozy within, and soon under the deft touches of Margaret's hands the home air began to grow.

As for the Stevensons, the season was so far advanced the staple crop of corn could not be raised on the farm, so a few vegetables for use were planted, and preparations were made for sowing

wheat later on. There being no house, John's first
care was to build one, in the meanwhile renting a
room in Burton till it should be completed. Very
soon a log house of two rooms was ready for occupancy, into which they at once moved. This may
not have looked inviting from the outside, for the
logs were rough-hewn, the spaces between the logs
or "chinks" were mortar-filled, and the great outside chimney hinted at comfort rather than beauty.
But inside! Ah, when the great fire began to
crackle in the capacious fireplace, as it did in the
early Autumn; when John, weary of his day's
work of digging, of plowing, came home late in the
evening to find a savory supper awaiting him, and
an earnest, strong face that lighted at his coming,
you would then have forgotten the rough outside
had you seen this, and would have exclaimed, "I
have found a home."

A rude stable was built for the faithful animals
that had journeyed with them, a well dug, and provided with a great "sweep" which lent a pictur-
esqueness to the scene. With these preparations
they considered themselves ready for the first winter in the West.

Just two miles distant was the growing, spreading town of Burton, constantly calling for workers;
here, when the weather prevented further work on
the farm, he worked that he might have something
"ahead" when the Spring should call him back to
the farm.

While the young husbands were busy, each at their chosen work, time might have seemed long and wearisome to the girl wives had it not been for the old sweet friendship which wonderfully brightened these first months of exile from friends.

Often when John was driving out Margaret would accompany him. Rachel would meet them both at the lane, and proudly escort Margaret to the cozy sitting room, where perhaps with laughter they would recall some incident of the long journey, or with tender regret talk of the dear old homes at Lynton. Before such a visit had ended, Margaret, with the air of a connoisseur, would inspect Rachel's great brood of hens, interesting because they were duty doing, as was evidenced by the goodly sum of "egg money" that came weekly into their owners' purse; or pay her respects to the family cow that furnished these farmer folks with butter and milk.

Then again Rachel, with a bit of sewing, would spend a delightful day with Margaret, when much the same program would be enacted. But there were stormy winter days and long evenings when each must stay by her own fireside.

These hours of enforced idleness might have been productive of what members of a later generation, when thrown upon their own resources, wearily designate as ennui. Not so at the farm. To them the earnest preacher had not preached in vain. Already they had begun to find a new world awaiting them in the few books which they owned;

besides they had come to find, as he had suggested, a welcome friend in their home paper. In it were helpful suggestions for farm and home, discussions touching upon every question of church or state, stories of travel and of biography, besides the weekly bulletin of the great onward march of the Church of Christ. After an evening spent around his fire side, reading aloud to interested Rachel and talking over with her the subjects discussed, this young farmer went about his tasks in a different spirit. He was no longer the plain individual John Stevenson, working out his own little problem of existence, but a unit of a great whole who by doing the duties of the hour, was unconsciously keeping step with the onward march of that great army which was ushering in a better civilization and bringing the world into harmony with ideals of its Creator.

More than once Rachel tried to tell her friend Margaret something of this pleasure, but the latter would laughingly say, "Oh Rachel, you are Jacob Ewing's own daughter, thinking more of a creed than of aught else," for like some others she refused to believe that a Christian literature could be other than a creed exponent.

Perhaps of all the old sweet associations at Lynton nothing was so greatly missed as the little village church. Upon coming to Burton our friends found that the settlers before them had taken pains at once to see that a place for worship was provided. So on a grassy knoll stood a little meeting house which like most of its associates, was built of logs. This differed in denomination from that in which our friends had been raised, but was one with it in the doctrine of right living.

Here every two weeks came a young and zealous "circuit rider," and on more state occasions "the Elder" of camp ground fame, who preached as was his wont of free salvation, and the necessity for immediate repentance.

On the very first Sabbath after their arrival in Burton, four church letters were handed the young minister and the little congregation almost startled them by the warmth of their western welcome. "Yes, there are some things different," Rachel was saying to John that night—and her eyes had a faraway look as the vision of the home church arose— "but these people are kind, and this is to be our home, so we cannot afford to be critical; perhaps we can make ourselves of use."

"Such a queer little church, and such odd people," was Margaret's comment as she and her husband together discussed the hearty hand-shakes and loud "Amens" of the morning.

"Still it is a type of this sincere western life of which we are now a part," rejoined her husband. "And," continued he, "as we cannot have our staid old pastor, nor be a part of his well ordered flock; neither is it right for us to live out of the church.

Therefore let us hope after awhile, things will not seem so strange."

Margaret made no audible reply, but there came echoing through her mind remembrances of many sayings of her father, as they had tramped about the farm, and in her *heart* she said, "It amounts to but little, after all."

By this first public step, both the Newtons and Stevensons became well known. As Rachel had said, kind hearts beat beneath the rough exteriors, and much interest was manifested in the welfare of the strangers, and on many an occasion a helping hand was held out.

The Newtons really knew nothing of the privations of frontier life, for William had a good position, while Margaret's patrimony had at once secured to them a comfortable home, but the Stevensons knew by experience every phase of homebuilding. Still they were young, strong and happy, each worked with a will, and by the time Spring had come bringing the ploughing and sowing, the humble log house had blossomed into a home. Much of the furniture was of the young husband's making. There was a stand very like the one in Rachel's old home, and on it was a family Bible very like its New England counterpart. Besides there was a steadily growing pile of carefully read books and papers.

One feature of the room, purely ornamental, must not be overlooked. Among the treasures Rachel had brought from her home had been an ivy root from the glossy green, which had crept and clung to the walls of the village church. This she planted in a rude earthen pot. Certainly western soil did not disagree with it, for it grew and guided over the little narrow window, spread itself, and growing covered the rough logs with a living beauty.

We will now leave our young friends for a time. It will be theirs to fight their own battles with the privations and experiences incident to pioneer life. We shall not look in on them again until many years have come and gone. We must not fail to chronicle the fact however, that by the time the old apple tree back in Rachel's girlhood home, had again scattered its sweet blossoms to the air, the Angel of Life had knocked at the door of each humble home. At the Newton's there was rejoicing over a son which the happy young father pronounced as handsome as his mother. In this he was not alone, for the numerous visitors, competent witnesses all, said "What a wonderful likeness; just his mother over again," but his appearance mattered little to the young mother who in a happiness of content of which she had not dreamed cuddled close to her heart sweet baby Richard. In the little log farm house, Rachel, too, could be found crooning a lullaby to a dear little morsel of humanity, a boy, who had John's own honest eyes, which even in its very young babyhood looked about quite as gravely as if life had already proven quite a serious matter.

But the mouth that Rachel kissed was very like her own, and it was not unlikely that something of her own nature lay hidden there. "What shall we call the baby?" This question remained unanswered, even until baby Richard began to look knowingly when his name was called. Finally it came the "Elder's" time for his quarterly visit. He had already gotten to call the hospitable farm house home, so of course he must admire the sturdy boy. Taking him gently in his arms he said, "And this is Francis Asbury is it?" And that night John wrote in the leather bound family Bible the chosen name, Francis Asbury Stevenson.

CHAPTER IV.

FIFTEEN YEARS; how much may happen, what changes occur in fifteen years, even when the conditions are settled; but in a new western town that length of time may stand for a half century in an older community.

Burton had moved forward like a young giant, and the summer of 1858 looked down upon a smart little city that was already fulfilling the expectations of its early friends.

Great rows of really good buildings lined the business streets. Comfortable homes, many almost luxurious, had largely taken the place of the log cabins of the past. On the knoll, still green and grassy, stood a neat frame church with slender spire, and rich-toned bell. The little log meeting house, itself the strongest factor in to-day's prosperity, has given way to its more dignified successor.

As a business center Burton was attracting the attention of many. The Illinois River upon which it was built not only furnished a sufficient water power for the mills upon its banks, and opened up communications with the rapidly growing interior towns of the State, but through its outlet into the broad Mississippi brought the markets of the great cities to the doors **of the business men of** Burton. **Besides this** two railroads, **with their snorting engines, now** connected it with **the East and North, and were** pushing on to the great western **beyond.**

For these reasons, and because of having been **first** in the field with its mill, Burton had become **a** center of supply **for** grain and flour. The little flouring mill into which **fifteen years** ago, William Newton **entered as an employee, had** trebled its **capacity.**

Let us, for a moment look in upon its counting room. There at the desk is the proprietor, **a keen**ly alert business man, upon whom **his** forty years sit lightly. We recognize the employee of other days, William **Newton, now** everywhere spoken **of** as one of Burton's most enterprising citizens.

Shortly after **his** arrival he had grasped the finan**cial possibilities of real** estate, and **making** some fortunate investments was able **to make** the first payment upon the mill, which was offered for sale. Once in his hands he managed its business so successfully that he became **its sole** owner, and soon became **known as a rich man to** whom the little world **of** Burton took **off its hat** in honor, after the manner of the greater **world outside.**

About a year before the reopening of our story, on one of the best streets his new home had been built. It was large and roomy, of brick, and stood in the center of beautiful, well-kept grounds. While a dweller in a modern house might miss some of to-day's luxuries and conveniences, yet comfort was evidenced on every side. Through the center ran a great hall, on one side of which doors opened into the large double parlors, whose side and folding doors were suggestive of merry companies of young people, or statelier and more dignified ones of older. From the other side of the hall one entered the "living room," and the large dining room beyond, and a great oaken stairway led on to roomy and sunny chambers above.

Over all this rules Margaret, the presiding genius of it all, the girl wife of long ago. In every graceful poise of the well-rounded form, as well as in the still regular features, is seen the maturing of the old girlish beauty.

Richard, the first born, is now a bright, handsome lad of fourteen, while a sister—Marie—has been his playmate for twelve years. Therese, the household pet is a petite little maiden of eight summers.

If fate has dealt thus kindly with those of the city, we turn with eager expectancy to the farm.

Though Burton had stretched itself out in nearly every direction, it had not seen fit to encroach upon the farm, so no fortuitious chance circumstance had come to the help of the inmates, yet by patient plodding, and self denying hard work on the part of both John and Rachel, every foot of the farm was now their own and unencumbered by debt or mortgage.

Anyone who has had an experience in laying out a home, or making habitable a wild piece of land, knows that ordinarily it is the work of years. Yet our farmer friends had been patient and willing to persistently plod, so necessary outlays were met as they came, and now, as we have said, the farm is theirs. Necessary improvements have been made, sleek cows graze in the pastures, and a great orchard back of the house is a source of enjoyment as well as of profit.

The improvement of the farm itself was more easily visible than that of the house, for the family still occupied the two original rooms of the log house, with two others which their growing needs had made imperative. A new home had been planned, but the one with farm experience knows that the comfortable home must come *last*. Yet though the house was of logs, it was often said there was not a more homelike spot to be found.

It is hard to analyze the something that makes a home. Yet it is a verity the stranger recognizes as he crosses its threshold, a something that alike draws those with a heart ache to its fireside, and the romping children of a neighbor as well. But whatever it might be, this farm home was certainly rich in its possession.

It may be the happy group of boys and girls it now sheltered contributed not a little to this home feeling as they romped over the rag carpet by the great open fire with its "backlog" and curious network of "firelog," and sputtering boughs of hickory.

Yes, the years had been fraught with changes, and among those apparent to even the most casual observer was the remarkable development of character, especially noticeable in the Stevensons. Not only for rugged, unflinching honesty was John known among his neighbors, but they had come to know that as he turned a furrow or sowed his grain, he did it intelligently, and many a one in perplexity learned to find a wise counselor in the quiet man, who betrayed by his conversation an unusual familiarity with matters outside his daily life. But it was in the little church which had so long ago heartily welcomed the strangers that John and Rachel Stevenson had grown to be most loved, most depended upon, for during all the years with a regularity equal to the coming of the Sabbath itself, the faithful team and light wagon bore the family to church. One of the recent innovations had been the organization of a Sunday school, and none could be found so capable for leader as the erstwhile timid John. And Rachel, with her years of quiet home reading was fitted to become a valued teacher, indeed, had she lived in these later years of woman's organizations she would have been seized upon at once as a "worker." It was curious to note the growing oneness of these twain. With

them the scriptural prophecy was being rapidly fulfilled. Perhaps the cause **of** this lay in **their quiet**
farm life, every detail of which was **planned to-**
gether, but we are inclined **to think it began in the**
long winter evenings, when after the roaring, crack-
ling hickory fire had begun to throw out its richest
glow the plain walnut stand was drawn out from
its corner, the candle lighted and the reading begun.
At first when the children were little they were
each tucked snugly away in their trundle bed.
(Years afterward they loved to recall how they
would **lie awake as long as possible listening to** the
rich cadence of their mother's voice, or to the
fuller, deeper, yet not less kindly one of their
father). When they became old enough it became
their pride, indeed a coveted honor, to take their
turn as "reader" for the **evening.**

Through these years a determination for the
higher education of their children had been grow-
ing, and had taken deeper **root** than even they
guessed. Together the parents **often** talked over
the means of attaining this **end,** and were finally
helped in the solution of the perplexing question by
a casual written suggestion. Acting upon this they
decided that on each child's tenth birthday **to**
present it with a cow, the sole profits from **which,**
as well as the increase, should form a "college
fund." This the parents hoped would not only
give the children themselves an interest in the

matter, but by the time they needed it, furnish means for an education.

They and the Newtons were still friends, but the growing dissimilar tastes of the two families were evident.

From the first, William Newton had been consumed by a desire to get on in the world; to this he bent all his energies. At first he liked to talk over with his young wife the affairs of the mill, but she laughingly informed him, "It was too dreadfully prosy," besides, she had no "head" for business, but would he not admire this delicate bit of her own embroidery she was fashioning for Therese or Marie? Left to himself he grew to live in a restless, rushing manner, borne down by the pressure of increasing business. He came hurriedly to his meals, and when he came home at night often the family had retired, unconsciously he grew away from them, and they from him. Margaret too had begun to find life a hurried matter, for the social honor and homage paid to the wife of a wealthy—and rapidly growing more so—business man grew very sweet, and society thrust upon her a hundred new duties. The great parlors became the social center of Burton, and many gay companies gathered there, for as a hostess she had rare charms. Besides she was really a loving mother with great pride in her beautiful children, and no hands could fashion so well the dainty apparel as her own.

What of their church relationship during all these

years?   From the first each, and especially Margaret, had been critical of the fervid western style, and
this feeling had grown with the years.   Had they
but kept themselves in touch and sympathy, as did
the Stevensons, with the great religious world outside, they would have recognized this with which
they were connected as but a unit in the great
whole, and so had patience with local peculiarities
and failings, but this they failed to do, and so during the years gave less and less of their sympathy
and drew more and more within themselves.   Yet
each Sabbath found them sitting decorously in their
pew.   **They** gave of their means for the support of
the church, but as to a self-denying sacrifice, to
carry forward the work, not one in all the company
of worshipers would have expected it.   So had
they found their place.

But we have tarried too long with the elders; let
us turn to the children, for with these our interest
centers.

Richard Newton was singularly like his mother
in appearance, with the same beautiful eyes and
mobile mouth, and a sunny, happy disposition that
made him the joy of the home.   From the time he
could barely toddle, his greatest delight had been
to visit at the hospitable home of "Aunt Rachel."
As he grew older, on such visits every nook and
corner of the farm would be explored, to say nothing of the great roomy cupboard with its possibili-

ties, or the cool milk house with its jars of rich cream.

Asbury Stevenson was of his own age, supple, strong and well built, and shy upon the surface. Between the boys there was that indescribable difference that marks the boy reared in the country from him familiar with town or city. Was there no other difference? Time will tell. These boys were good friends, but it was Louise, Asbury's sister and junior by two years, who was Richard's born comrade, and who accompanied him upon every exploring expedition, no matter how perilous. She was a plump little maiden with brown hair that rippled back from her forehead, good eyes, and a sunny, cheery face. Yet if she, in her plain gingham slip in which her busy mother dressed her, had stood for a moment by the side of dainty Marie Newton in her garniture of frills and embroidery, not many would have called her beautiful.

But her mother knew a strong soul was locked up in the little breast.

From the first Louise became the constant playmate of her brothers. Did they climb the loft to search for the hidden nest of Old Speckle, Louise could spring as nimbly up the ladder as they. Did they play marbles? Louise soon mastered the mysteries of "mumblepeg," and her shot was as unerring as theirs. A tomboy? Well, perhaps she was. Yet mother was beginning to depend more and more upon the swift feet that almost flew upon her errands, and her marvelously sweet, low lullaby often soothed the younger ones, thus bringing relief to her mother.

As has been said, she and Richard were born comrades. When he was but six and she four they played at housekeeping with all the dignity of elders: In childish disputes as whether the "house" should be under the old apple tree, or the great elm, Louise's strong will usually won. Sometimes this capricious little girl was well pleased at the result. Again she would say, " What did you give up for?" "Because I had to," retorted Richard.

"Maybe if I was a boy I'd give up, every time," Louise would rejoin contemptuously.

Asbury was from the first a quiet, studious boy, and loved nothing so well as to hear his mother read, or as he grew older read for himself. Besides he and Louise, four other children had come to bless the home. Ruth, a quiet little girl of ten, and Edward and John, two sturdy, strong, sinewy little fellows still younger, and baby Rose, not yet a year old who, accepting the logic of events as any healthy baby in a large family soon learns to do, lay in her crib crowing at a fleck of sunshine that filtered in through the little window, or with a strangely serious air studied a set of pink toes which insisted upon discarding socks, a happy, healthy baby, requiring and receiving no care beyond its natural wants. Rachel had begun to show the effects of these years of toil and anxious motherhood, yet such

was her executive ability that the domestic machin-
ery moved with less jar than in many less well ordered homes of smaller family, for each child had
its appointed tasks which were performed without
question.

By means of this method there was time not only
for church, but for the evening with books as well.

*   *   *   *   *

Having now noted the changes wrought by the
years, and the influences that are at work to mold
the children that gather about each hearthstone, we
again leave them for a little space, knowing that
the harvest of seed-sowing is rapidly ripening, and
the inevitable reaping must quickly begin.

CHAPTER V.

CHARACTER STUDY.

IT WAS a bright sunshiny morning in May, 1861, eighteen years from that other May day when the two brides had gone out from the village church when the two families met at the hospitable farmhouse in honor of the anniversary of the event. How the great long table groaned under its steaming and tempting burdens! How the children, the younger ones at least, raced and romped over the farm!

The two older ones of each family were at school in the "Academy," but they were out to-day ostensibly to do honor to the event of long ago, but in reality to have a jolly day together on the farm which continued to be to the Newton young folks the greatest pleasure imaginable. We may as well pause here to explain that the Academy was an institution of which the people of Burton were beginning to take a just pride, and which they owed to the far-seeing intelligence of the very early settlers. It had grown with the growth of the

town until now it had begun to attract the young
people of the country and neighboring towns.

Asbury and Richard at seventeen, and Louise
and Marie at fifteen, have outgrown the old-time
scramble down the straw stacks and up into the
roomy mow, but there was the great swing, and
just far enough for a delightful tramp was the
shady piece of woodland, rich just now in its wealth
of spring violets, buttercups and sweet williams.
"Oh let us go to the woods," exclaim the young
people, and a little later are searching among the
outlying roots of the trees for the flowers that
nestle there. And we who are watching them observe that as Richard gathers the choicest of these,
he shyly gives them to the cheery-faced, light-
hearted girl whose voice, as she has walked by his
side on the tramp, has gaily carolled snatches of
song as sweet as that of the thrush on the bough
overhead.

After the bounteous dinner John and William—
the latter having snatched a few hours from his
business—took a stroll over the farm, for what
seems more like a creation fresh from the hand of
God than does well-kept meadows and hillsides
after spring breezes have blown over them? So
thought at least the hurried man of business, as he
drank in the quiet rural scene, and something like
regret crossed his mind at the contrast between this
and his own hurried rush for gain. But no; he
could never be content with the slow, plodding life

of the farm. Rachel and Margaret lingered in the cozy sitting room for reminiscences of other days. But each in her way was too busy a woman to dwell long in the past. The growing interests of their homes and children had pushed the past farther and farther back.

Just now they are discussing a question of evident interest, about which there is evidently a disagreement.

"No I cannot consent to such a thing." It is the clear, firm voice of Rachel that speaks.

"And why not? What possible harm?" And there is a shade of annoyance in Margaret's tones.

They are discussing a dancing school which has lately been opened, at which Margaret Newton has placed not only Richard and Marie, but little Therese as well, and she is urging Rachel to do the same with at least her older children.

"Much harm every way," Rachel rejoined, "As I see it; but, Margaret, we have gone over this question in some shape so many times, it is hardly worth while to reopen it." Yet Margaret continued,

"You know I do not favor—no more than you— the public ball, but for your children and mine, with perhaps a few other neighbors' children, to dance together in my home or yours, is no more harm than—than to swing together," she concluded as her eyes fell upon the creaking swing just outside.

"If children went no further than their parents expected or intended, your argument would be good," said Rachel. "But do you remember Hazel Run, at Lynton, which began in a clump of hazels in your father's farm, but became a noisy cataract in Rocky Hollow a few miles distant? How can you know but that when your children are older, and the world bids for them remembering that dancing and card-playing—I believe you give it the more genteel name of eucher—received the stamp of home approval, they may leave your marked-out home restraints as surely as Hazel Run left *its* quiet beginning. Besides," she continued, "if there were no other reasons, the Church has labeled such *questionable*—"

"The Church!" Margaret broke in vehemently, "such restrictions are obsolete, behind the times. Are you the only right interpreter of the Church? Dr. Heron's children will attend this school, so will Judge Gibson's, and what would the Church do without them when it came to meets its financial obligations?"

"Deny—" but Rachel's rejoinder was cut short by the return of her husband with Mr. Newton.

These had lingered to discuss the site of the new house, the stone for whose foundation already having been hauled, and which was to be begun as soon as the summer's work was lain by.

As they lingered, too, they had talked earnestly of the gathering war cloud now about bursting over the land. Like an electric shock but a few weeks before, pale lips had passed on from one to the

other the sentence, "Sumpter has been fired upon!"
And even now as these two old friends talked,
came the awakening martial strains of drum and
fife, and close behind the hurried tramp of an army
which had sprung as if by magic from the work-
shop and the farm. The very first tocsin had been
strangely thrilling to John Stevenson. But yesterday at a mammoth "pole raising," he had been one
to float to the breeze at Burton a bright new flag,
and not one in the crowd would have guessed that
the still, quiet man who so steadily adjusted the
fluttering ensign, was longing to snatch it and rush
to the front of the battle.

"I must buy up all the grain I can," said William
Newton. "There are going to be heavy demands."
Through such different glasses did these two men
view their country's needs! Then, after a moment's
thought, William Newton bent over and asked the
other a question, and that other answering a little
confusedly, said, "after Rachel and I have talked it
over." Then turning they entered the house, inter-
rupting, as we have seen, the discussion between
Rachel and Margaret. Once there the all-absorb-
ing "war talk" became general, and continued till
the departure of the guests.

"Mother, I want to join that dancing class," was
the announcement Louise startled her mother with
as they were busy about the evening's work.

"What do you know of the dancing class?"
asked her mother, in order to gain a little time.

Then it came out that both Marie and Richard had painted in glowing colors the pleasures and advantages of the school.

"And mother, Mildred Gibson and Will Herron are going and I want "—"to do something because some one else does?" queried her mother. Then tenderly, lovingly she went over with her daughter the reasons why she did not wish her to do this. But it was not easy for Louise to give up that upon which she had set her heart, and only on account of the habit of obedience that she at length became willing to yield her will and trust to the judgment of her mother.

The conversations of the day show in what different directions the children of the two families are started. Both in the same church, yet with what different feelings are they taught to regard its obligation. In one its restrictions are considered irksome, which are to be ignored or condemned as foolish; in the other, these are shown by the tender voice of the mother and the no less kindly counsel of the father, to be at least safe and in the end helpful. In the one self gratification had been eschewed from the cradle, and the happiness of living for others enforced by precept and example; in the other usually, a want was but to be made known to be gratified.

But outside of the parents there was yet another molding force at work. In the Newton home stood an elegant book case filled with well-bound books,

really a good selection, too. There were books of
travel, most of the poets, handbooks on some of the
sciences, and a few cumbrous volumes of history,
yet they stood so prim and methodical one knew at
a glance they had been read but a little. It was
true, the Newtons had never been a "reading family;" that is, there was no regularity in their literary
habits. There were the books, perhaps first one
member of the family and then another would take
down a volume and browse as fancy might dictate,
but it remains a fact that to arouse an interest in a
book it must become a family affair, be read aloud
—at least its choicest passages—and discussed.

Yet this implies a certain amount of leisure, an
unknown factor in the city home, for business
claimed the father, and on most evenings, society
the mother. Indeed with the years each child
came to have its "engagements," so that few evenings found the entire family home. Yet, they read!
Ask Marie and Therese! Under their pillows,
stored away in their drawers, were novels of the
most sensational type which they had learned to
devour. Alas for the hurry; alas that at this form-
ative period of their lives, there had not been one
with leisure and inclination, whose pleasure it might
have been to open to them the great field of
thought which would have broadened and deepened
them, and perhaps bound them with silken fetters
to the Church of God. Had there been one such
what sorrow might have been averted.

The reader already knows that in the other home with which we have to do, humble though it was, books and papers had from its founding been a strong factor. The impress of these has been seen in the father and mother. It is becoming quite as visible in the children. Louise would not have so readily yielded in the matter of the dancing school had not her young heart been loyal to the church, made so, largely, by the books, magazines and papers which had recorded its triumphs, as well as the devotion of its servants. Indeed, even the parents did not suspect the depth of this silent, constant influence.

*   *   *   *   *

Night had fallen upon the sunshiny anniversary. The children of the farmhouse, worn out by a day of unusual pleasure slept soundly, but the parents lingered to talk over the events of the day, a surprising one of which Rachel now learned, was the confidential request of William Newton that inasmuch as he desired a sum of money to invest in the immediate purchase of grain to meet the extraordinary demand sure to be made, John should become surety for the same. The idea was not relished by either, as anything savoring of debt was peculiarly distasteful, but there could be no danger, both agreed, for Newton's far-seeing business instinct had become almost a proverb.

Rachel regretted the growing estrangement which the day's conversation had indicated. Might not this be an opportunity to bridge over the growing chasm?

"Yes, it had better be done," was the decision. This settled, the conversation drifted back to the threatened war; its probable length and extent was discussed. Suddenly there flashed upon Rachel a realization of the heartache all this meant. In her mental vision she saw the sad farewells of husbands and wives, the going out of brave young boys who had been the joy of home. Was it strange a wave of thankfulness that her eldest was so young? Arising, she went softly to the bed where Asbury lay sleeping and gently kissed his forehead. "No *my* treasures are not demanded," she softly said.

Oh, blind Rachel! Was there nothing to whisper aught to you of the battle waging in the faithful heart so near you? Can you not read the dumb agony written in the eyes, that just now are so curiously watching you.

CHAPTER VI.

THE WAR—AN ACCIDENT—LOUISE AND RICHARD.

THE next few months slipped by with startling rapidity. On the farm heavy crops had been harvested, and lumber was ready for the new house, which John seemed strangely loth to begin. At the mill, William's prophecy had been fulfilled. The business had certainly quadrupled. Instead of the war cloud blowing over, as many had hoped, it gathered in intensity. And in these first few months the Nation seemed in the throes of dissolution, as news of continued defeats flew northward. This became the absorbing topic—all else dropped into insignificance.

One evening in the early Autumn, John Stevenson sat reading the "Daily" which in these troublous times had suddenly grown to be a household necessity. Suddenly he threw it aside, with the remark, "Another call for volunteers." Something in his voice caught his wife's ear. In a moment she was by his side, her arms about him. "You— you— surely you don't think—" but she could not

5

finish—only to gasp, "Oh! the children!" Gently he told of his long struggle, how **duty** seemed urging, **nay** driving him **to** the **front.** "And **what a coward!** How the **children, and even yourself, would have a** right to blush **for me if I failed my country in** this supreme hour **of** need." **As he talked,** his face lighted and glowed with **the thrill** of patriotism, and with breaking heart, and ready intuition, Rachel perceived how useless would be a protest against his heart convictions.

For answer, she silently bowed her head upon his **breast. With a** lightning-like flash **she** saw the **weary years ahead. No** more sweet counsel together. **Upon her alone must rest that burden.** Somehow, she must take upon herself the management of the farm. And then—Oh, dreadful thought —so many had marched off never to come back. They **had** died **in** battle, on the wearisome march, or of wasting disease **in** hospitals.

Could she **stand** it? *Ought* she to? Ah, but **there** was the bleeding Nation and **its** strong, iron **willed** President calling for **brave men.**

Other women's hearts were breaking: why not **hers?** She lifted her head, and her husband knew her heart had said "Aye."

A few **days** later at the supper table William Newton announced "John has enlisted." **He and his wife** talked much of the unwisdom of the act, **but in the** heart of each, there was a respect for the **brave soldier** which neither cared to acknowledge

to the other. "His regiment is about full and he
will go to the front in another week," Newton
added as he left the room.

How readily we adjust ourselves to the inevitable!
A week ago the sun had shown so brightly and as
Rachel remembered, in a dazed kind of way, she
had been so happy when Asbury had come home
from the Academy but a little while ago, and announced his promotion, as a reward for some extra
study he had been doing. Could such a small
thing ever make her happy again? With hardly a
sigh the plans for the new house were given up.
So does a greater grief absorb our lesser ones.

The last few days were given to the hurried
preparation of some articles necessary for the comfort of the dear one. At first the grief of the children knew no bounds. Asbury, proud in his
seventeen years, begged to accompany his father;
but no—the mother was firm—*that* sacrifice had
not been demanded of her.

Louise went to bed dreaming of hospitals, band-
ages and of broken limbs. Could the mother have
looked into that warm impulsive heart, she would
have been surprised at the ambitious plans brood-
ing there. As for Ruth, it was touching to watch
her as she silently followed her father about the
house, watching an opportunity to slip her hand
in his, or cuddle in his lap. They had always been
peculiarly knit together, and for them the parting
promised to be hard.

On the day following his decision, he was surprised while at the barn to hear childish sobs above him. With a swift, silent step he reached the mow; there prone on the hay lay little Ruth. "Father, Oh, father! we will die without you!" he heard her sob. In a moment he had gathered her to his arms and tenderly, as though she had been older, he explained the grave needs of the hour, then added, "And my little girl may help by praying each day and night for my return." After this there were no tears, but the faithful little body followed him like a shadow.

The last week slipped by—surely never had a week hurried so. The last morning dawned, clear, bright, beautiful. As Rachel mechanically opened the blinds she noticed as much, and that the early frosts were scattering the leaves from the great elm. Already there seemed a pathos in the tossing of the bare limbs. "It is as well," she murmured to herself, " Let them toss and moan if they will as Winter's blasts fall upon them." " 'Tis but a type of life's emptiness."

John was to leave before noon, and before the home adieus were said he went mechanically to the barn, ostensibly for a last word with the hired man, but in reality to take leave of the animals that for so long had been a part of his life. Black Nell that had faithfully helped to draw the great wagon westward so long ago was no more, but Princess, her daughter and counterpart, stood contentedly in her stall, and gave a low whinny of recognition and rubbed her nose against the arm of her master. But time was passing, and voices on the outside were calling. John paused a moment at the stall of "Superb," a great stallion noted alike for his strength and at times for his viciousness. Why does he chafe so? What is that about his hoof? Ah, in his pawing he has loosed a board, and see, a nail has been thrust in the hoof. To see anything wrong, with John Stevenson, was but to try to remedy it, so with a "Stand still, there, Superb," he entered the stall and stooped to adjust———.

It was well that the man who was to help on the farm opened the barn door just then, for a sharp moan went up, then all was still. A few minutes later Rachel saw them bearing a still burden straight to her door. Five minutes later Black Princess was galloping rapidly to Burton for medical help. Rachel's husband was seriously injured if not killed, and as he lay back upon the pillows it looked the latter. Outside the door were grouped the frightened children. Asbury had flown to Burton for the doctor. Louise had grasped little Rose, and not knowing what she did, began humming a nursery ditty. Poor Rachel, utterly stunned, with a heart that seemed suddenly to have become lead, walked first to the bed, then to the door to look anxiously down the highway towards Burton.

The jaunty blue soldier's cap lay on the floor where it had dropped from the improvised litter.

Mechanically she picked it up, and there rushed in upon her a realization of what was to have been, and what was.

But it was left for Ruth—timid yet practical Ruth—to go softly to the bed, rub the cold hands and bathe the brow till a low moan told that he yet lived.

The physician gravely shook his head. One cruel stroke of the great hoofs had broken a limb, while another had injured the spine, it could not be told how seriously. For a week the father lay between life and death, and while he so lay, the "Company" that was to have been his marched away. Two days before their departure Rachel went to William Newton and handing him a roll of bills said, "If my husband lives he cannot go. To do so was his heart's desire. Take this money—we had saved it for a new house—get two "substitutes" in his place; the Country needs them, and the log house will do." Brave, patriotic Rachel! There were thousands like her. Can we of a younger generation ever appreciate the sacrifices of those terrible days?

* * * * *

It was found that John Stevenson would not die. He would live, for a time at best, a semi-invalid.

While he is being nursed back to health we must again look in upon the young people, and another visit to the Newton home becomes necessary.

It has been seen that the older ones of each family were in the Academy. But teachers and parents found it hard to hold the young mind down to study. Outside was the roll of drums, and "news from the front" was the all absorbing topic. In all this as a matter of course, the boys became intensely interested. In every village, town and hamlet, "Companies" were formed, a captain chosen, and the "common" became a drill ground where youthful patriotism huzzaed itself hoarse. Burton had its Company, and after its marches and countermarches, usually its young Captain would be led to a goods box from which with youthful fervor he would orate upon the day's struggle. This, was Richard Newton, who seemed born for leadership. Hearing the huzza even the busy William Newton would smile, for his "dream" lay in his handsome boyish faced Richard. The late investments of this man of business had surprised even himself by their quick returns, but he found fortune a stern mistress. He must make no reservations if he would serve her. When his soul rebelled at the bonds he would comfort himself saying, "The strain will soon be over. I shall have amassed a great fortune and then—." His wife, always a doting mother, as she perceived Richard and Marie slipping into manhood and womanhood, determined that they should have every advantage that money and social position could procure.

The young people of Burton had learned to love the great roomy parlor and spacious dining room beyond, for in them, charming evenings had been spent, now in the "harmless" parlor dance, now at the low whist tables; both Richard and Marie had become skillful players at the last. When the proper hour would arrive, Margaret, the gracious hostess, and Marie, daintily gowned, would serve the refreshments.

The Newton grounds boasted many trellises of the choicest grapes, and under the supervision of the mistress herself, each year casks of home-made wines were stored in the cellar, which were drawn upon for these same refreshments, and usually it was Marie's own hand that poured the rich liquid. Yes, what with music, dancing, cards and wine, the evenings did pass gaily.

It is true some parents shook their heads, but then "the Newtons were so eminently respectable." Besides, Mrs. Newton was a known society leader and as such was often heard to express her strong disapproval of public dances, only could they be allowed in the parlors of home or friends. When one suggested that "cards" belonged by right to the saloon or brothel, her reply was, "boys had better learn at home, so there would be no temptation to assail them when they were out in the world." "As for wine," here her lip would curl comtemptuously, "as if one could not control their appetite! It would be a weak person indeed who could not sip a glass of home-made wine without becoming a drunkard." Yet even now, could she have caught the whisper, it was beginning to be said outside the home that the handsome son of this woman who felt so sure of the correctness of her views, was already becoming too fond of his cups.

Margaret Newton prided herself upon the fact that she was "progressive." It was a favorite saying of hers that "we ought not to try to hold our young people down to the notions of half a century ago, and as for the church! well, if the church would hold its young people, let *it* modernize."

It was strange that among the molding influences that shaped this family, the contents of the handsomely carved bookcase did not exert a greater influence. Strange, too, that among all the elegantly bound books there was such an utter absence of any specifically religious. No, not strange, if we recall the elder Richard Allen and his seed-sowing, and the truth that the harvest is greater than the sowing.

But among the young people of Burton there was one family whose young people had no part in these social evenings at the Newtons. We say "young people of Burton," for though the Stevenson farm lay two miles distant, yet so closely were the inmates associated with the church and school, indeed with all the interests of the town, that for all practical purposes they were a part of it.

From the anniversary day, when Rachel Stevenson had so clearly expressed her convictions, it had been understood that while at other times the

Stevenson boys and girls were glad to be at "Aunt Margaret's," on these social evenings they would be absent. With Asbury and Louise, who were but wide-awake, fun loving young people, there was at times not a little dissatisfaction over this decision, but from babyhood they had been taught to obey, so in this they yielded to the judgment of father and mother. But upon Richard, accustomed to have his own way, this decision fell the hardest, for from the days when he and Louise had played at house-keeping beneath the elms she had been his comrade, his boyish ideal, nor had dawning manhood changed this, and to be thus preemptorily deprived of his. old-time playmate was unendurable. But Mrs. Stevenson remained firm, so while the Newton's danced in their lovely parlors, making the evenings gay with laughter and song, Louise, Asbury and Ruth took turns in reading aloud to their invalid father, or studied the lessons for the morrow.

CHAPTER VII.

ACADEMY LIFE AND HOME EVENINGS.

THESE were months of anxiety and care to the Stevensons. Going back to the day when the father was carried in so nearly dead, the broken limb easily healed, but continued excruciating pain revealed the fact that a serious injury to the back had occurred, and it was months before it was known that he would ever again walk. Twice came the sowing, and twice the reaping, before he was able to creep forth, leaning upon his staff, seemingly an old man.

During these months of his invalidism Rachel suddenly found herself face to face with several problems, which unlike all others which had arisen could not be settled by mutual counsel. One the question of the farm management, another involved in that one was, should Asbury and Louise remain in the Academy? Each was strong and well built. Would it not be wise to have their help at home during this emergency? For the first few weeks after the accident, while the others slept, she, wide awake, turned over each side of this question, which she felt must be settled for the future rather than for the present.

"No" she finally said, "they must remain in school at all hazards." So the trusty farm hand who was to have staid during her husbands absence at the front, was retained. The younger boys were now sturdy lads, and these with Ruth became more than ever their mother's helpers, remaining at home during the first winter, reserving though, certain hours for study and recitation to either Asbury or Louise. This seemed a necessity, for the invalid required the almost constant care of his wife. Outside of school hours Asbury and Louise lent willing hands, but they were nearing the final years of the academical course, and their studies required much time; besides, it was her father's earnest wish that Louise should devote as much of her time as possible to music. Her voice, a rich mezzo soprano, had about it an indescribable touch of pathos which strangely touched the hearts of all who heard her sing. Richard Newton, it may be said, sang too — a deep, musical tenor—and sometimes as these well chorded voices rang out together from the plain sitting room a curious fear smote Rachel's heart and unconsciously she found herself paraphrasing Rebekah's old lament, "What sorrow to my soul, if my daughter take a husband of the sons of Heth." But she brushed it aside. "They are but children and have played together from the cradle."

So with work, with planning and with some anxieties the days of John Stevenson's invalidism went by.

"Rachel," said he one day, while he was still in the bed, "has Newton ever said whether or no the note for which I became security has been paid?"

"No; but I must go in to Burton this afternoon. I will see him." An hour later she was interviewing the rich owner of perhaps the most prosperous mills in all western Illinois.   •

Now, while the investment for which Newton had borrowed the money had proven successful, still there had been so many wonderful "openings," the sum had been reinvested again and again. Just now it was out, but next week it would lie in the bank and a stroke of his pen would cancel the note. This much he explained to Rachel. "But I would rather it was paid," said her husband when the message was given him, "go to him again, and tell him I cannot allow my name to remain longer." His long confinement was telling on his nerves, Rachel thought, still this message was taken and William Newton bowed in acquiescence and John felt a relief, as did Rachel, that it was "settled."

During the last winter of the convalescence, an event occurred which on account of its bearing upon the two families must not fail of being chronicled. A great religious awakening occurred. Beginning in the church where our friends worshipped, it spread throughout the city. Its effects were wonderful in the Academy, nearly the entire school being converted.

With the Stevensons, **each child had in their** infancy been presented for baptism, and later **on,** after careful instructions in church doctrines and usages, had been received into full membership in accordance with the plan of their church. To neither of these children had it occurred that anything further was necessary. Yet again and again **came** the reiterated message from the lips of the earnest preacher, " Ye must be born again," follow**ed by** the **strange altar scenes, where** amid tears, **prayers and songs, a face would** suddenly brighten **and glowing with a strange light, would** exclaim, **" It is finished! "**

Louise had never doubted but that she was a child of God, as indeed she was, yet she was the first among her brothers and sisters to feel the need of something which as yet she had not possessed, and in her own impulsive way, without a word to **the** home folks, she knelt at the altar where she poured out her young soul in prayer. Presently a strange peace stole into her heart. She remained yet a little while upon her knees, then arose with the joy born of the conciousness of Christ Spirit within illuminating her face.

Oh, young, impulsive, warm hearted Louise! could you have seen the **weary years and heartaches** ahead, the heavy trials that await you, the work *He* has for you, you might perhaps have lingered longer to pray that through it all this new found joy and peace might always be yours.

It was a matter of comment between the father and mother during these meetings that Asbury took little or no interest in them. For awhile he had been regular in his attendance, but finally contrived to stay away upon one pretext or another. One night, after the family had come home from church and had fallen asleep, Rachel was awakened by a noise in the little bed room where Asbury slept, and a voice calling, " Father, mother, come here!" Each hastened with a fear of sudden illness. What was their surprise to find Asbury up and dressed, and *in tears*, and to be met with the exclamation, "I must have this question of Salvation settled now."

With tender and tactful inquiries both parents sought to find the difficulty. Born, and baptized, and brought up in the Church, taking a delight in her worship, well read in her literature, grounded in her doctrines, still there was a hungering in the soul, a burden on the heart. The hortatory style of the preacher had aroused a conviction of personal un-worthiness. For weeks the burden had grown heavier, till now it was unbearable. Fortunately, from earliest childhood religious talks between chil-dren and parents had been common, so there was none of that shrinking timidity which at such times frequently drives the seeker to some other than the family. Grasping the situation at once, the father got his Bible, and both he and the mother began to point out the Scriptures, making plain the wondrous plan of salvation, showing that there must always be an individual surrender, a giving up of self, an acceptance of Christ as a personal Savior.

Suddenly there came an illumination of the mind. The wondrous simplicity of it all dawned upon the struggling youth, and while his mother's voice was going up to the throne, he exclaimed, "I see it all!"

> "The great transaction done,
> I am the Lord's, and he is mine."

And now it was John and Rachel Stevenson's turn to be surprised. Could this be their quiet and reticent boy, who with beaming face was shouting aloud, praising God till the brown old rafters fairly shook with the echo?

Old-fashioned? Yes, perhaps; but it was that blessed old-fashion that throughout the ages has made the church strong and stalwart, that has implanted and nourished such clear convictions of right and wrong, that at a word armies have sprung into existence to do battle for the right. The old-fashion that has sent pioneer preachers and teachers to the western desert till it has blossomed as the rose, has sent out missionaries till from heathen lands news is wafted of a nation being born in a day.

And quite as necessary as any of these seemingly greater results, has planted in every church, no matter how humble, those who uncomplainingly become the burden-bearers, and in their daily lives are living witnesses of their Master's power to save.

During the remaining weeks of the meeting none were so earnest and none more successful than Asbury Stevenson.

Nor were the Newtons left unmoved. Indeed it could not have been otherwise with the religious feeling so intense. Asbury's conversion was hardly less a source of joy to the Stevensons than was that of Richard Newton. Indeed, Rachel seemed to rejoice even more than his mother, who said carelessly, "Of course I knew the children would identify themselves with the church. Religion is right and proper, but should not be carried to extremes."

It is one of the strange things which we meet with in life, that a mother frequently allows herself to become absolutely blinded as to her children's morals and habits. Now that Richard was nearing manhood his mother did not seem to notice that for her son the old home evenings had lost their charm and more and more, upon one pretext and another, he was coming to spend these away from home. He usually made a feint of going to his father's office, but there there was but little to interest him, for he knew really nothing of the business. Besides his father in these last few months was growing really nervous and irascible, and to wear a haggard and worn look, and seemed ready to find fault, with little or no provocation, with his pleasure-loving son.

6

Yet if the office atmosphere was not pleasant, there was no need to seek far for hearty goodfellowship. Burton had changed rapidly since the old days of log houses and stumpy streets. It had already begun to ape metropolitan airs in many ways, and alas! to reproduce city vices with startling exactness. So in brilliantly lighted rooms where the clink of glasses was often heard, together with coarse laugh and jest, and steady click of the billiard balls, Richard occasionally dropped in for an "evening." More than once Marie, whose room adjoined his, with a pale, startled face had seen him come home, staggering, maudlin. Did she tell his mother? No, for one of the gifts of the years to Mrs. Newton had been a set of "nerves" that absolutely forbade her being bothered with anything disagreeable, so Marie kept her grewsome secret. Did Mrs. Newton know nothing of the state of affairs? No one could tell. Perhaps pride kept her silent, but more likely faith in the Devil's choicest saying, "Let him alone; he must sow his wild oats."

Yet if his mother kept sealed lips, Dame Rumor did not, and it became current among his acquaintances that "Young Newton was going to the bad." Bits of this rumor could not fail to reach the Stevenson home. Here Louise, with the old imperious stamp of her foot, declared it all false, every word of it. So Rachel carried a double burden—real sorrow over the misdeeds of one who had grown up as one of her own flock, and misgivings about the future of that one of hers who so ably defended the sinner. Therefore it was with extreme satisfaction the Stevensons heard of Richard's conversion.

They had yet to learn, as do we all, that while grace does much for a soul, it cannot take the place of careful training, and that the modern Christian sower finds, as did the one in Galilee, that not a little of the results of his work withers away in the burning heat of every day temptation.

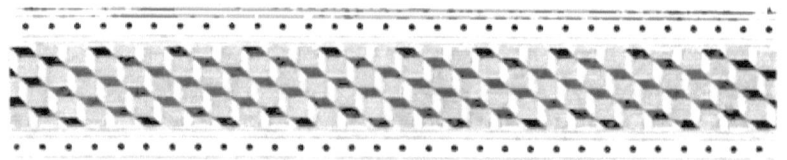

CHAPTER VIII.

ASBURY'S DECISION.

EIGHTEEN hundred and sixty-five! What memories are evoked in the hearts of many by the bare mention of this date! During all these months and years since John Stevenson's Company had marched away without him, the great bloody conflict had been waging. The Nation had lived at fever heat, the ordinary affairs of life were forgotten in the excitement of "news from the front." Slowly, though, within the last few months the war cloud had been lifting. Rumors of peace were afloat, finally came the news of Lee's surrender, and soon the steady tramp of thousands of returning brave men shook the streets of cities and aroused country hamlets. How the lusty cheers went up from some of these last, as little groups of bronzed veterans came marching down the streets. Usually the fleet telegraph had announced their coming and then they were welcomed by the citizens with the wildest enthusiasm. Alas! that in the midst of this joy there should have been so many black robed figures, who wept because not all who had as bravely marched away, came back. At such times Rachel Stevenson's heart ached for her husband, for the pallor of his face and the tightening of the lips told how great the trial of invalidism instead of active service had been. Patriotic as we have seen the Stevensons to have been, and therefore interested in the close of the war, still the year was to be fraught with events of direst moment to the family.

In June Asbury was to be graduated from the Academy. It had been hard during the closing years to hold him down to study. Once when a specially urgent "call" for troops had come, he had insisted upon going. To this his mother emphatically said no. "You are too young for efficient service" she would say; adding "There are just as truly battle fields ahead. God would have you prepare yourself that he may use you where He will."

As the event of his graduation drew near, both he and his parents, each in their way were considering his immediate future.

It soon became evident to the "home folks" that Asbury was carrying a burden. Like many another mother Mrs. Stevenson had found that there is an age when it is not wise to follow a boy, or question him too closely; besides this son of hers had inherited from his father a trait which made him more difficult of access—concerning that which he felt most, he said least. So daily she prayed for

him, but felt he would be stronger if some questions
were settled without word of hers.   One thing she
rejoiced in was that already, as the result of the
"college fund," dating back to the gift of the cows
when he and Louise were each ten years old, there
was now on deposit a sum sufficient to insure each
two or three years at a University.   With that
much secured, somehow the rest would come.   So,
if he chose, a higher education—both her own and
her husband's ambition for their children—awaited
him.   But to return to Asbury.

One day about a month before his graduation he
surprised his mother by coming home during school
hours.   " Why, what is the matter; are you sick?"
queried his mother.   " No," and he passed into his
room.   That evening at family prayer, he said,
" While we are all together I may as well tell you
I have settled it."   "Settled what?" came in chorus
from his brothers and sisters.   But his mother, who
with an anxiety all unknown to her child, had
watched the struggle from the beginning, arose and
walked across the room, and putting her arms about
him said, " That you are to preach the Gospel, is it
not?"   For answer there was a tightening of the
hand clasp, tears fell from his eyes and his head
bowed assent.   Yes since the memorable night of
his conversion he had carried about with him the
constantly increasing burden.   "Woe is me if I
preach not the gospel."   Now he had rolled it off
in unquestioning obedience.

How quickly affairs adjust themselves to suit new conditions! Within a week after Asbury's announcement, it had been decided that after a summer spent in helping on the farm he should enroll as a student at a University in another state.

This University, in addition to its excellent theological course, had a comprehensive course, open alike to girls as well as boys, and after much consultation it was further decided that Louise should forego her last year in the Academy and accompany him, but none could tell whether or not Louise was happy over the arrangement.

This being an interwoven history, we must now return to Richard Newton.

For a while after his conversion, already three years in the past, his life had been exemplary, but who can estimate the force of habit, or thwart the power of molding influences in childhood? Although in a sense he had been brought up in the church, and had now voluntarily united with it, still he was almost entirely without reverence for it.

He had heard criticisms concerning it, its requirements scoffed at, disregarded. Besides he, and his sisters not less, while boastful of intelligence on other matters and proud of the cultured surroundings of their home, were really ignorant in regard to it. Its glorious past with its splendid line of achievements was utterly unknown. As for its current history, indeed this family knew less than of the most trivial political affairs in Europe. How could it be otherwise when the books upon the library shelves were of art, science, poetry and fiction, but *not* religion. The magazines that monthly loaded their center table were rich in serials portraying society well, with its loves and hates. They often contained beautiful gems of thought, instructive articles, but of the church they were silent except as some question was discussed philosophically.

Mrs. Newton was an enthusiast over flowers; her windows glowed with green and crimson, even on the chilliest day. How carefully she read her horticultural magazine that gave her needed information. Mr. Newton could not have lived, so he thought, without his favorite political paper, but in all their family life a paper devoted to the church, giving its current events and general progress, discussing its questions of interest, had not been considered a necessity. So with the father engrossed in other matters, the mother with prejudiced notions concerning culture and society, it was not strange that these young people in their efforts to become Christians should find great difficulties.

Knowing nothing of anything more, the church at Burton was to them *The Church.* If Deacon B. deviated from the correct path; if his wife were shrewish, or took an undue interest in her neighbor's affairs, this became an argument against the church. If the little company was more zealous than cultured, these æsthetic young people smiled in a patronizing way and gave "the church" a discredit mark.

The well read young people of the farm well knew that back of all these was a long line of illustrious scholars, poets, statesmen and orators who had been proud to give their allegiance to this same church.

Then there were the *habits* of these young people. Their feet were nimble in the dance, their hands skillful with cards, they loved the taste of their mother's rich home wines, and had been trained to think all this *right*. It was little wonder that erelong Marie and Therese, though retaining a nominal membership, relapsed largely into the old life.

What of Richard? handsome Richard. His was really a noble nature, and his heart full of lofty ideals; his ready wit and genial ways made him a popular comrade. We have seen him as a boyish orator, firing the hearts of an improvised military company. His chosen literature were the great speeches of Webster, and of Patrick Henry.

One of the great events of his early boyhood had been a debate which had been held in his native town between Illinois' two great sons, Stephen A. Douglas and Abraham Lincoln. His father had smiled at his boyish enthusiasm, for he had followed the speakers' every movement, had edged his way among the great crowd quite up to where Lincoln stood, (it was on the stump of a great tree in a neighbor's yard), and no gray head drank in the

keen cut, irresistible logic more eagerly than he.
"Ah, well," thought the proud father, "who knows
but he too may win honor and fame some day?"

Yes; he made a noble effort to rid himself of the
habits he had formed. The last two years of his
academic life were given to hard study. Such was
his brilliancy that he soon seemed to have made up
for lost time, and his teachers said "what a reformation!" They did not know, nor did even keen-eyed
Rachel suspect the secret that, stronger even than
his love to God, was the growing, deepening love
between himself and Louise, and that by this
slender, silken cord this young girl was drawing him
away from the evil into a sincere desire for the
good.

CHAPTER IX.

A LOVE AFFAIR AND A MOTHER'S VIEW OF IT.

DIMLY the old brick walls of Burton Academy loomed up that June evening in the dusky shadow of the moon. The trees in the campus were laden with their heaviest foliage, and the drooping branches cast shadowy outlines upon the winding walks over which little groups of students, mostly in twos, sauntered in the moonlight. It was commencement week, and the evening of the college social. The walk led up quite near to the building, where it divided, leading up to the two entrances, leaving a triangular bit of ground, filled with the choicest flowers. Just now the air was heavy with the rich wealth and fragrance of masses of June roses. Among the shadows on the great stone steps, sat a young girl and her companion. In her lap lay a cluster of roses she had gathered in passing, the petals of which she aimlessly scattered as the low, earnest tones of her companion fell in sweet cadence upon her ears.

It is the old, yet ever new sweet story, which

shall never lose its freshness till the last son and daughter of Adam has quitted this earth.

"Listen, Louise—" Ah, it is Richard, eloquent, love stirred Richard, who is speaking.

"You must hear me, for this may be our last opportunity together, for I am sure your going to college is but a plan to separate us. I know too well I am not a favorite in your home. How can I be, when our family notions of life are so different?" And then with all the hot, impassioned fervor of youth he pleaded his love, and for the sweet promise that should indissolubly link their lives together.

Little need, Richard, had you but known it, for all this eloquence. The treasure you seek is yours. The link you ask for has been forging through the long happy hours of childhood. The opening years of young manhood and young womanhood have strengthened it. Indeed, who shall say that in the great councils of your creation and hers it was not said, "What God hath joined together let not man put asunder."

As his words died away a little hand crept shyly into his. The June breezes murmured softly around the stern old walls. The flowers but a step away lightly touched their heads together as if in knowledge of the sweet secret, but the young pair were silent, for vain are words to voice the tumult of a soul.

They could linger but a little while, for during

the evening Louise was to sing. Poor Louise! How could she face the audience? Surely her precious secret must be read by everyone, and it was in a strange, bewildering maze of happiness with which presently she joined with Richard in the long promenade of the hall. And Richard, happy, audacious Richard; more than once he looked down into the bright face at his side, and boldly whispered " My Darling !"

Once on this promenade they passed Rachel, who sat chatting with some friends. Something in the air of the couple suddenly arrested her attention and sent a momentary pang to her heart. "They are but children," she said to herself. "Louise will forget all this in the coming year at school." Presently the rich voice of her daughter rang out in song. The selection was a light, joyous one, and surely never did lark or linnet on swaying bough warble so joyously, nor did ever an upturned feathered throat anywhere so surely sing of joy and peace.

Rachel listened in wonder as did the audience, but no voice whispered to her soul of the new experience of her daughter. How strange that often we are so slow to read the hearts of our own.

This mother had watched this young girl grow from her own arms, first into the toddling, willful, vivacious child; afterwards into the loving lightener of her own cares, and later into the peculiar sunshine of their home.

She had grieved at times over the imperious will

and had rejoiced when she had deemed it laid low at the Cross. Yes, she knew her so well, every trend of her mind, yet had one hinted to her that this child might carry a woman's heart in her breast, she would have resented the idea. Still more would she have been appalled could she have guessed that this same heart had awakened and responded to that strong, strange emotion whose coming is but nature's signal that the gates of childhood are forever closed.

As for Richard, "boyish Richard!" she had said to herself more than once lately as his fondness for Louise's company became more marked. Had it not been his delight all his life to rummage her cupboards in search of cookies and toothsome sweets; had not he and Louise led in mad pranks all over the old farm? No; it was but the veriest nonsense to think of him as her daughter's lover. Yet following uncomfortably close upon this conclusion came the remembrance of the lover-like looks which had startled her, and against her will she found herself, surrounded though she was by music, flowers and a gay crowd, calming her newly aroused fears with arguments why Richard Newton should *not* be her daughter's lover.

Not only the half hushed whispers of his own personal shortcomings swept in upon her, but the worldly, irreligious life of the family. It had been to her a source of real regret that the old sweet ties of friendship had been gradually yet so surely loos-

ened, that now each family had come to be well
content to "gang their ain gait;" that which one
family held most dear and sacred, the other considered not at all worth the while of people of culture.
Indeed, it had often seemed of late that Mrs. Newton took special pains to flaunt or parade her own
easy notions of home life in contradistinction to the
sterner code of the farm.

"There can be but one end for all this," Rachel
had more than once said to herself, "and that is
complete shipwreck of the Christian faith and the
complete engulfment in the vortex of a purely
worldly life." "No, it must not be!" and her lips
closed; and they who knew her best would have
known an appeal from that decision would have
been useless.

During the homeward drive John Stevenson and
his wife talked of the music of Louise's song, of the
heavy growing crops on either side of the highway,
but never once did Rachel think it worth while to
mention her newborn fears. Besides, if there was
any growing feeling between the two, happily she
had decided how it could be best managed. That
very evening she would await Louise's coming,
would calmly, lovingly point out the possible dangers and insist upon a halt in the boy and girl
friendship. "How glad I am I thought of the
danger in time," was her satisfied comment to herself, as with book in hand she sat down alone to
await Louise's coming.

Meanwhile the two lovers were loitering on the homeward drive. We shall not obtrude—let the soft sheen of that same old moon which has lent its witchery to so many such scenes, and the wafted perfume of June roses and leafy verdure be the only setting to this old yet ever new story which ardent youth pours into willing ears.

Lofty plans are made for the future, for hides there in all the world an obstacle which does not vanish on the approach of that old magician Love? So says all the fairy lore of the past, so believes the youthful pair who so slowly ride on. It is well that the illusion is so complete, for in the coming years one weary heart at least will pause in its tireless work for others' weal and in remembrance whisper, "surely Heaven can be no sweeter." But there is a patient watcher whose strained ear just now catches the rumble of wheels, then the sound of a low good night at the door, and Louise has entered the room.

As her feet crossed the doorway, involuntarily the watcher's lips quivered slightly, then tightened. She was firm.

"Why mother, are you still up?" the musical voice called out.

How beautiful she was that moment! even her mother, burdened though her heart was just now with a perhaps unpleasant duty to perform, could not but let her eyes dwell on the dainty picture. The soft folds of her simple evening dress fell about her. In stature she was undersized, but her form was perfect and had a willowy suppleness that lent a peculiar charm. But it was in the mobile earnestness of the face which portrayed every passing emotion, and in the liquid softness of the eyes wherein lay the greatest charm.

As she stood looking down at her mother she caught her wistful, tender look which unawares had stolen into the upturned, questioning face. Ah! how many times she had been cuddled in those faithful arms, how many times that work-seamed hand had smoothed away her troubles! Why should she not now tell of her new happiness? Dropping suddenly upon her knees in her old impulsive, childish fashion, she laid the soft white hand in that of her mother's, exclaiming brokenly, "Oh, mother! Richard! I am so happy!" and the brown head nestled in her mother's lap.

Had a thunderbolt fallen at her feet, Rachel could not have been more surprised. A half hour ago she had sat waiting to kindly, yet firmly point out a future possible undesirable result, and now that dreaded result was a fact.

What should she say? Should she call up her motherly prerogative of reproof and forbid the affair entirely? Ah, she knew the strong, unyielding will too well for that. Swifter than did ever a modern telegraph ring out an alarm, the cry for help went straight to the Throne, and with the cry was borne in the message, "take time." Yes, she must have

7

time. Time to think it all over, to use all the tactful resources of her nature.

For answer she kissed the sweet young face, saying, "Another time we will talk it over; just now I cannot take in your evident meaning. Surely 'tis but a boy and girl fancy."

"Mother!"

The young girl catching the unfriendly tone, had arisen. In that one word Rachel, in weariness of heart, recognized that the *child* was forever gone, and a woman with whom she must battle was in her stead.

"You must sleep now," she said, "another time we will talk it over," and putting her arms gently about her, led her to the little plain room she shared with Ruth.

It was long before either slept. With Louise her mind dwelt first on her newfound happiness, and again on her mother's strang reception of it. "She thinks us children! Oh, mother!" and the very tone of the thought implied a constancy that boded ill for Rachel's plans.

And Rachel; for hours she tossed upon the bed, and feverishly asked herself the question, "How can this foolish boy and girl affair be stopped?" for that it must be stopped was as clear to her as noonday. But how? And until the early morning hour she still asked herself, "how?"

The next day bade fair to be an uneventful one. The mother still felt herself unequal to the task of

discussing the matter. She had not even yet told
her husband. Louise, in the shyness of young girlhood, avoided all mention of it. The shadows of
the afternoon had already begun to slant when
Rose still the baby pet who liked nothing better
than a romp with Richard came in and triumphantly announced that " Richard had come, and was
talking to father."

The hot crimson blood surged up to the very
roots of Louise's hair, for on the evening before
Richard had told her that before another day closed
he meant to stand before her family as her accepted
lover. " It will be so much better," he had said,
"to have the matter clearly understood." The
plans for the future of the young pair were yet
misty. Richard had already in a desultory manner
begun the study of law, his chosen profession, but
lately he had thought much of a position with his
father in the mill, and a cozy home for his young
bride. But even if the future was not settled, in
his frank way he was determined his new relationship to Louise should be known.

Hearing he had come, Louise sought refuge in
her own little room, and Rachel nerved herself for
she felt that a crisis was at hand. The door opened,
admitting her husband and Richard. On the first
face was written perplexed surprise, with not a little
alarm. On the other, oh, what a metamorphosis!
Strong, manly resolution had succeeded the boyish

smile. It dawned on Rachel that the "fancy" had taken deep root.

"Mother," her husband always spoke thus when a matter of importance was being discussed, "Can you guess what Richard has asked of us?"

Rachel cast a swift, searching, almost pitying glance upon the eager bright face.

There was no fear of her in Richard's heart. All his life she had been to him a kind of second mother. He had gone to her with a want as readily as to his own. True, he had said to Louise that on account of different family views of life he was not a favorite, yet love had made him bold. Surely there could be no real opposition from her who had known him all his life.

So in an instant he had gone to her side. "You know I have always loved Louise. I thought it only right to tell you that we have pledged our mutual love, and we shall be happy with your blessing and good will." An oppressive silence followed, broken at length by Rachel, whose voice sounded strange and husky.

You know, Richard, that we would willingly make any sacrifice for Louise's good, but I am surprised that you should seriously ask this; you must know that you are each far too young." Richard made a gesture of impatience. "Your education is incomplete; so is hers; you have made no plans for the future; it would be a positive unkindness to you both for us to consent to what you ask. In a few years you will each laugh at this passing folly."

A flood of anger rose to the young man's face at these words.

Just then he caught the flutter of a dress in the room beyond. In a moment he was by Louise's side. "Come, my darling, we must settle this together," and impetuously he led her into the room where sat her parents. What was it that caused her to seek her father's side? Mayhap in that swift instant she read a growing heart tenderness. Certain it is, from her mother she expected no pity.

"Passing fancy!" It was Richard who spoke. "I tell you I verily believe this love was born in me. I could give up life easier than I could give up this. As for further education, Louise's love will be an inspiration. As for life's plans, we will be willing to wait, if we must, but such men as have had a loving heart by their side are those who have made the greatest success of life."

How well he pleaded his cause, Rachel could but think.

"Can *I* ever be happy? Can my daughter ever be happy, if she takes a husband from a careless worldly family? Aye, if reports be true, a husband who has already learned to love sin; the first flush of love's young dream over, would he not grow weary of her sterner morals? Ah, might not these morals tone themselves down to the lower plane?"

No, this alliance must never be. She must speak plainly.

"Richard, your notions of life are different from ours, as are your ideals. What to us is the most sacred, to you is a subject for jest. When Louise is older she will see this for herself. Until then I must think for her."

This young man in all his life had known but little opposition, and now to have this supreme wish disregarded was unbearable; besides Rachel's last words had touched him as the others had not.

"And for such a cause you would part us! And yet I am to admire such religion!" "Louise," and he turned to the young girl, "have you not a word to say?" For answer, without looking at her mother, Louise arose and walked to her lover's side and calmly put her hand in his, turning such a look of unutterable love upon him that a wave of happiness swallowed up his anger.

Rachel bowed her head while a very storm swept over her. Was this the reward of motherhood? Was it for this she had known no other law than that of uncomplaining self denial? And she knew that in this clash of wills she was right. Thus far the father had said nothing, though keenly alive to every phase of the disputed question.

Turning to his daughter he asked, "How old are you Louise?"

"Eighteen, my last birthday."

"Mother," said he, "time has been cheating you;

Louise is no longer a child. Just so old were you when you left your father's roof to share this humble home with me."

His wife could scarcely believe what she heard. Certainly he did not approve what to her seemed unendurable. Louise quickly appealed, "Father, we are willing to wait if you think best, but help us to settle this that there be no estrangement."

"It seems to me, mother," added he gently, "this need not be settled definitely now. The young people have said they were willing to wait. Let Louise go with Asbury as we have planned. Let Richard prepare himself for life, and then—and then, mother, after all, this is something each heart must settle for itself."

These words seemed so reasonable that even Rachel, as well as Louise and Richard, felt it was best to acquiesce.

It was hard for matters to drop back into the old groove, indeed Rachel feared more than once the old sweet intercourse between herself and Louise was forever gone. Richard, with lover-like boldness, did not make his visits to the farm fewer, but insisted on coming and going with his old freedom. Meanwhile there was a growing good comradeship between Louise and her father.

But to be fully employed has been a cure for many a heartache. So the busy days at the farm-house served to tide over what might have been an embarrassing time. Asbury was doubly busy, for

his father depended largely upon him and the
younger boys for harvesting the crops. Besides
he was studying that he might enter an advanced
class at college. Louise, too, had her full share of
work, so the Summer went by.

Richard had had yet another experience after his
first interview with Louise's parents, the details of
which he could not unbosom even to Louise, but
which had given him much food for private reflection. Straight from the farm he had gone to his
father's office. He had gone with a vague expectation of asking for a partnership in the business, or
for a position with a salary. Entering the office to
which he had grown more and more a stranger, he
caught sight of his father at a desk. How weary
and care-worn he looked! How hot and stifling
the air!

Some how, after a sight of the bowed figure, it
was not so easy to begin. Yet after a few common-
place remarks he began his story. Rachel Stevenson's surprise did not exceed William Newton's.
But yesterday he might have answered him gruffly,
but to-day, with that handsome, glowing face before him, how could he? But a partnership? No,
alas! A position with a salary? No. Father
and son talked long and earnestly over the ledgers,
and at the close of the conversation the father went
back to his accounts with a sigh. The son passed
into the sunshine with a preoccupied air. When
he next saw Louise he told her he believed his
fathers advice best, and that he would enter a
school of law that coming Autumn.

CHAPTER X.

COLLEGE—A STUDY OF HOMES.

LAZILY the first hint of September breezes played in and out of the open door of the farmhouse.

Within there was far more hurry and bustle than was common to this well ordered home. Rapidly the mother moved about, placing now and then a forgotten package in one or the other of two trunks which stood almost ready for the final straps. Outside by the gate, champing their bits impatiently, stood Princess and Nell with the familiar light wagon which was to bear Asbury and Louise to the train which in turn was to whirl them to that world of new experiences, the University.

As their father drove up, an involuntary pain clutched at their mother's heart. How often this selfsame team had driven up in their childhood to carry them to church, to school, and now they were going. Was it forever?

The morning prayer had been full of pathos at the parting, and rich in pleading for Divine care. Yet this mother could not see them go without a personal prayer for each. So alone in the little chamber she knelt, first with Asbury and then with Louise. With trembling voice she prayed first that life and health might be spared, and that each should make the most of the opportunity that was to be theirs to fit themselves for wherever duty might call.

Then followed a hurried parting, and soon the footsteps died down the gravel walk, and the two had gone out from the home.

How strangely silent the house seemed to Rachel, who was left alone. While their going was the fruition of her hopes, still it was borne in upon her as she listlessly went about setting things to rights, that her children, as children, were gone forever. If their lives were spared they would return only to go out again, finally to take their places among life's toilers.

She recalled their childhood, their peculiar dispositions and their probable future. How her heart thrilled as Asbury's exemplary life arose. How clear his brain; how studious his habits; how unflinchingly he had walked in the path of duty.

And Louise; she had been a good daughter. Throughout her whole life her willing hands and feet had lightened her own cares, while her cheery, bright ways and sweet voice had made much of the home music. As for Richard, with her husband she had come to think that had best be left to time, and that surely time would settle it aright. He had left the week before for a college farther east, and she trusted that new faces and new associations would break the tie.

A few hours and the family had returned, and the routine of work and study was resumed. Ruth and Edward were each in the Academy, while John, a sturdy lad of thirteen, with little Rose attended the school nearer home. So the house much of the time was strangely quiet, and very unlike the old patter and bustle of busy feet.

On the farm matters were assuming a more cheerful financial outlook. The rich pastures were flecked with cattle. The dark prairie soil harvested good crops. Long ago good barns had been built, which now in the Autumn fruitage, were filled to overflowing.

One of the maxims of this family had been the scriptural injunction, "Owe no man anything." So now, as the father had gotten much stronger and the younger boys were old enough to relieve him not a little, the Stevensons rightfully looked forward to a greater leisure, for the farm, while not a means of rapid wealth, is surer than most others.

Since the abandonment of the new house at the opening of the war, the subject had not again been broached, only as something in the indefinite future. But now it was planned that when Asbury and Louise should come home for the summer vacation they would be welcomed to the new home, nothing elegant or pretentious, but added room which would make household cares less burdensome.

So much time has of late been given to the farm-house that it is high time that we were turning to the more pretentious home of the Newtons. We have already seen the old friendship wavering under the strain of growing uncongenial tastes, in addition—but perhaps they fancied it—both John and Rachel thought since the refusal to remain longer on the note as security Mr. Newton had been strangely reserved even to the point of avoidance. Moreover, Rachel's known hostility to the affair between Richard and Louise touched Margaret as perhaps nothing else had, for in Richard's love for this sweet, blithe girl her mother heart perceived his strongest safeguard, and her selfishness could see nothing amiss in the sacrifice of innocent young girlhood upon the altar of a hoped-for reformation.

Yet, if a growing fear lurked about her heart, the years saw no change in her home life. Home wines were still found in the cellar. She refused to see danger lurking in the amber-colored, quivering jelly which bore the pungent flavor of choice old Burgundy, nor in the brandied peaches upon her cellar shelves.

Nor did she think it worth while, now that there were young Christians in the family to attempt new reading habits. Another might have argued that these should be supplied with a literature which in itself would foster and develop the new experience and bind them irrevocably to the new life; not she. She had lived a life of moral rectitude, why not her children? She did not ask more than a moral life for them, so she knew no regret when Marie and Therese lapsed into the old worldly life, nor but little uneasiness when Richard at long intervals came down to the morning meal with aching head and dull eyes. Had not even some great men been a little wild in their youth? She received with extreme satisfaction his ready acquiescence in his father's wishes for a college and law course. She was sure he would come home crowned with honor.

Marie had yet another year in the Academy. She had always been a beautiful child, and was growing into a lovely young womanhood. Her heart and impulses were good. In an humbler or Christian home she might have developed into a strong womanhood; as it was, she became a type of thousands who sacrifice everything to the demands of dress and society. She could "play" a little on the pianoforte, but of music as an art, a life study, she had not dreamed. Had she known the first elements of hard work and patience, she might, in time, have done something as an artist; as it was she was content to paint what her young friends styled "perfectly lovely pictures," and then smiled.

Like her type, she would probably marry early. Indeed in the home circle her "engagement" to Charlie Hudson, "a good fellow," and what was better the son of Banker Hudson, was already acknowledged, but the marriage was not to occur for a year. Once married she would become, in all likelihood, a conventional society woman not unlike her mother.

Therese was something of the same pattern, yet there was a certain dash about her that gave one a sense of uneasiness akin to that which a restless team imparts, not knowing exactly what turn it may take. She was a winsome girl, about the same age as Ruth Stevenson, and between these two a warm friendship existed. From earliest childhood she had been inordinately fond of reading. She it was who eagerly cut the magazine pages to devour its monthly dish of "serials." She had a keen literary perception, and had she had a faithful guide into the sweets of poetry or the wealth of history, or had she been directed even to the better class of fiction, how much of sorrow would have been averted. As it was she was left largely to follow her own inclinations. To do her mother justice, when she perceived this growing and absorbing taste, she did try to check it. As well try to dam a stream and leave the fountain untouched. So Therese grew to live more and more in the realms of fancy, often imagining herself the heroine of whose woes she was reading. No wonder she found the church irksome, the home dull, and the plodding studies of school life unendurable.

Standing in life "Where the Brook and River

Meet," unconsciously to herself she was beginning to long for an exciting experience akin to that of the heroines whose exploits she found so thrilling.

Before we leave the Newton's to look after the students whom we left rapidly whirling college-ward, we must look in upon Mr. Newton himself. To do this, it will be necessary to seek the office, for he is scarcely at home, except to hurried meals, and at late hours for slumber.

Though scarcely fifty years of age, his hair is rapidly whitening, the old-time sprightliness of step is gone, yet the eyes maintain the old alertness with the addition of certainly a trace of feverish anxiety.

Since the days of his first speculation in Burton real estate he had lived a restless life. Through the troublous days of the war he had so success-fully managed his large interests that his fortune had doubled and trebled.

He had always been a loving husband and indul-gent father. Nothing that money could devise to make the home happier was lacking, hence there never was a thought but that the family purse was unlimited.

Within the last year Mrs. Newton noticed with anxiety that he was becoming more and more ab-sorbed in his business, and taking on a haggard and preoccupied air. She had never been lacking in wifely devotion, and it was with forebodings she began to expect a breaking down of his health, and to urge him to take time for recuperation, but instead he seemed to apply himself even more closely.

Mrs. Newton and her daughters were still punctilious in their attendance upon the morning services at the church, but it had come to pass that Mr. Newton scarcely ever accompanied them. Indeed he found no day so free from interruptions, consequently none so well adapted for work on his ledger. So Sabbath after Sabbath this overworked man of multiplied cares sought to untangle the chaotic threads of the past week's work.

But were they chaotic? Not once did Mrs. Newton suspect this, but such ugly rumors were rapidly gaining credence. As a drowning man rapidly divests himself of any burden which hinders his life struggle, so it was apparent that William Newton was drawing his business affairs into a narrower circle.

Still the ponderous wheels of the great mill swung around with lightning rapidity. The furnace fires glowed brightly, and the huge chimneys were black with the cloud which overhung them night and day.

There was certainly no signs of decay about that busy hive, and if aught of the rumors were true, it was compelled to remain a rumor, for the lips of the proprietor were closely sealed, and his bearing as self-cofident as ever.

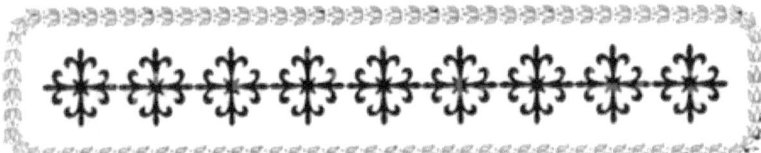

CHAPTER XI.

DEVELOPED CHARACTERS.

IT WAS with mingled feelings that Asbury and Louise found themselves at the last moment hurried from the quiet of the home, upon the journey which was to open to them the coveted new life. Keen regret was felt as the reflection obtruded itself upon even their young minds, as it had upon their mother's, that the old home life was forever gone.

But just ahead lay that wonderful future called "Life," whose successes and failures so surely awaited them, and before which intervened a few coveted years of college life. And as each recalled the self denial of the family life, the hard-working father and mother, it seemed marvelous that the dream of years was being realized. So it might be forgiven them if with the natural regret was mingled not a little proud exhileration and joyous expectancy for the life ahead.

This was particuliarly true of Asbury. All his life he had been naturally studious. The quiet home evenings had been rich in their implanting in his mind of broad plans for the future, for during these had been developed an intimate acquaintance with men and women whose lives had shaped church and state, and as the acquaintance grew, his young heart had beaten in unison with their struggles and triumphs, and unconsciously had grown up the desire to also live for a purpose, making some little corner of the world better for his having lived in it. Then had come his conversion. Again, the still, solemn promptings of the Spirit, which knew no rest till he had given his life to the service of his King. And now he was about realizing his desires. Little wonder that the past rapidly melted into the glorious future.

Louise, though in a different way, shared his enthusiasm. The parting between herself and Richard had been full of mutual hopes and pledges for the future, and though years should intervene before the fruition of their hopes, still they were young and strong in each other's love, so the parting was without bitterness.

And though she began her collegiate course with a tumult of heart of which staid Asbury knew nothing, yet it was with real girlish enthusiasm that she too found herself journeying collegeward.

The journey occupied a day and a night, and after a few hours the dainty lunch was gotten out. How welcome the flaky bread, how delicious the home butter, and what motherly remembrances

had been exercised in preparing some specially
liked delicacy. About dusk the following day the
travelers found themselves at the end of their
journey.

They experienced a momentary shade of disappointment as they stepped into the fitful, weird
light of the platform. How small the town; but
each remembered it was the University they had
come to seek, and the great noisy crowds of young
men and women proclaimed it a University town.
Trunks came tumbling off by the dozen; old friends,
jolly comrades of the past, called out to each other in
noisy and exuberant greeting. Yet if the many
were thus at home in their surroundings, not a few
stood hesitatingly, not knowing just which way to
turn. Among these last were Asbury and Louise,
but not long. They soon found temporary lodging
for the night, and the next day found them settled.
Asbury to room near the college, and Louise in a
home farther away. Acquaintances were rapidly
made, the college course was studied, each was
classified and student life began.

It was indeed a delightful experience to awaken
in the morning, absolutely free from care. No
waiting, insisting breakfast to be gotten, no hurrying that the burdensome dishwashing might be
gotten rid of before school, no lowing stock to be
fed and watered, no horses to be curried; in short,
perfect freedom from the old exacting cares, with
time to study, time for exercise, with the environ-

ments constantly tending to bring out the best there
was in one. Here was an entire community of young
people, all, with hardly an exception, earnestly
at work. At home, in the Academy, both Asbury
and Louise had been known as the "best students,"
but here they soon found that if the old order of supremacy was to be maintained, hard study was
before each.

Perhaps in no place in which one finds himself,
is the aristocracy of intellect so apparent as in a
college. Wealth, social position, even the cut and
material of one's clothes, matters but little, but the
essential question is, "are they good students?" It
took but little time for our young friends to demon-
strate this question to the satisfaction alike of faculty and students, and they were soon received into
the inner sanctum of good favor and fellowship.

So well had Asbury improved his time at home,
that after his examination he found he would have
but three years in the college. He hoped for an
additional year or two for special preparation for
his life work.

Louise, it will be remembered, had yet another
year in the Academy, so she felt well satisfied upon
being admitted to the freshman class, where she
soon became known as a hard-working student.
Her sunny disposition that had made sunshine
in the old farmhouse, as well as her ready helpfulness, soon made her deservedly popular. Added
to these traits was her clear, rich voice, which soon

made her presence at social gatherings much sought after.

No, Louise Stevenson did not go to college as a recluse, to dream of nothing but her absent lover, but rather as a clear-brained, wide-awake girl, who meant to get as much as possible out of life. Yet soon her most intimate friends came to feel that with them all there was a reservation which outsiders did not penetrate, for Louise was faithful to her absent lover.

Though her mother was building much on the new scenes that were to break the fatal spell of early love; with Louise such scenes could come. She could even grow to be a strong factor in these associations, yet even as the needle points irresistibly towards the North star, quite as surely did the soul of this earnest and sincere girl cleave to the absent. Poor anxious mother heart! You may as well know now that there is nothing which will sever this tie. Nothing? Hold; there is a pure brave heart in that girlish breast, there is clear knowledge of right and wrong, more, a hatred of wrong, and there is a *will* strong enough to lay down a life or a love if right should so demand. Closely should the absent lover watch his actions lest they be the power that breaks the sweet tie.

Among the new friends Louise had made, her room mate, Emma Ward, grew to be one of the most valued. Her home was in a distant eastern

city. She had been born into an atmosphere of
Christian culture and wealth. She had seen this
wealth held simply as a means providentially given
to help in the problem of the world's betterment,
and one of her earliest lessons had been that the
possession or non-possesssion of wealth by the individual might be a mere incident of circumstances,
but that back of this in determining friendships
should be the solid rock of personal worth and
character, and hence although in the Ward mansion
the petty economies and hard work with which the
Stevenson young people were so familiar, were
unknown. Yet the ideals were the same. In the
mansion, quite as truly as in the farm house was
God loved and served, so it was not strange that a
warm personal friendship sprang into existence, a
friendship that came to be far-reaching in its effects
upon Louise.

Emma had been in the college the previous year,
so had not about her the shyness of the newcomer.
She was known as a good student, yet not particularly brilliant. Moreover she was of a bright, fun-
loving disposition. From the first hour of meeting
she was strongly attached to the shy country girl,
and when one Sunday evening in the privacy of
their room, Louise began with her marvelously
sweet voice to sing some of the church hymns so
familiar in both homes, the work was done, Emma's
homage was complete from that hour. As for
Louise she began to be drawn out of her-

self and to really enjoy the social side of college life.

* * * * *

But there is yet another student in whom we are interested. Richard Newton had left for college with emotions far different from any he had before known, emotions little guessed by any of his home circle, save his father. To understand these it is necessary to go back to that morning when, angry at the unexpected opposition of Louise's mother, he strode out from the farm house determined to lay his plans before his father. It will be remembered that after this interview he had gone out silent and oppressed, and strangely willing, considering his natural impetuosity, to abide by his father's suggestions. Let us go back to that interview. As this prematurely old, care-engrossed man who like many another had lost his family in a sea of business, looked into the handsome glowing face, there swept into his heart a vision of the old days at Lynton when he had wooed and won the beautiful Margaret. Patiently he heard the story to the end, but the remorselessly keen eyes gave no trace of tenderness as he sternly said:

"You are barely twenty-one, not yet out of school. You have no profession, nor no notions of business that I have ever been able to discover."

Richard winced. Yes, he had often declaimed against the irksome confinement of the office.

" Do you think it wise to take a wife to poverty?"

"But father, I see my folly; give me a small humble place in your business."

"My business!" bitterly interrupted the elder. "Come with me;" and there in the curtained alcove, the place where Mr. Newton spent so much time with his books, Richard caught his first glimpse of the bankruptcy which like a threatening sword hung over the entire Newton interests.

"We may avert it for a year," continued the father, "but if you are wise you will go to college while you can, get a profession and be ready for life."

"Yes, it is the inevitable," thought the stunned Richard, "I will go."

The college selected was one of the oldest and carried the proud prestige of being one of the most influential in all America. Long lists of its alumni were holding positions of honor and trust throughout the country. While this remained true, yet some other matters were not so satisfactory.

While there was a class of hardworking, painstaking students who were making the most of their opportunities, there was a large "crowd," or several "crowds," who spent their evenings in bacchanalian revelry, and among the unsatisfactory results was the fact well known and widely commented upon, that many students went out from this proud institution utterly wrecked in morals.

Richard upon his entrance was soon a favorite. He entered with energy upon his studies. His fine physique and manly appearance won for him many favorable comments, for even at that day athletics were coming into prominence. Then he had a certain boyish artlessness or frankness which strongly appealed to the heart. His natural oratorical powers soon came out in the society meetings, so it was not long till it was decided that he would be an addition to any " set."

He had gone to college with such manly resolutions. Perhaps these latter might have been helped had he chosen a college, or rather if his parents had chosen for him one which had cared less for prestige and more for the morals of its students, one that did not fear to stand before the world as a distinctively Christian institution. But of this we shall see.

CHAPTER XII.

RICHARD AND LOUISE.

IT is a fact that in every college, however small or great, there are at least two "crowds" or "sets," oftener more, and much of a student's success depends upon the set with which they become identified. So wrote a wise editor, and so one morning shortly after her arrival read Louise, and reading it she laid the paper down to speculate upon the truth of the statement. Yes, it was true; even her short experience told her as much. There was even here, she recognized, though held in check by the high moral character of the institution, a set bound by ties of congeniality, whose watchword was "fun and a good time." If they could only have fun, no price was too dear to pay for it. Yet there was another, and these made up the majority, who were hard-working and painstaking, reaching results not attempted by the gayer crowd.

Into which had these young friends of ours fallen? They had been hard-working at home, they were not likely to choose idleness now. Their sweetest associations outside of their home life had been found in the church. They naturally turned to it now, and ere long these two became known not only as careful students, but consistent Christians as well. Louise in the meanwhile helped and broadened, as it is not hard for us to guess, by the companionship of that refined, cultured young Christian, Emma Ward.

Asbury naturally took his place among the young theologues. His roommate, Earnest Warren, was like himself a divinity student, yet from his predilections it seemed not unlikely that he might eventually find his niche as a teacher of the sciences he loved so well. His home was in the State of Ohio, and his family of the "plain people," who had economized that their son might have that lever denied to them, an education. After this glance at the associates of Asbury and Louise, with whom it is safe to leave them, we turn to ask what of those of Richard Newton.

Among the great body of students was one Will Braceton, a fellow of rugged, robust build, and withal of a good mind. He might have easily led his class in any study, had he chosen, but he chose to be the leader of a set which was itself a leader in most of the mischief which a wild, fun-loving crowd of unrestrained young fellows could devise. Had they been contented with mere mischief it might not have seemed so bad, for that can be forgiven, but it was no uncommon thing

for them to gather in Braceton's room, or
some place of his appointment, drink wine, and
sing senseless bacchanalian ditties. Yet much of
this was not known outside of the company, and
with many Braceton stood for much that was
good.

A few weeks after the opening of the school
year, at one of these "evenings" in Will's room, he
suddenly said, "I tell you what, boys, that Richard
Newton is all right. We must show him every
possible attention and win him for our crowd."

From that hour Richard had no need of homesickness, for there were patronizing friends at
every turn, and very soon the character of the new
friendships became too evident. Richard's past
experiences instantly warned him of the danger
lurking in the proffered friendship, and he was
brave and firm in his determination that he would
allow nothing to interfere with the steady course of
hard work he had marked out for himself. Ah,
had it not been for that caged demon of appetite,
which having been fed and pampered into existence,
angry at its whilom confinement, revenged itself
now by wild periods when it clamored to reassert
itself.

Yet without special incident the months of the
college year sped by with astonishing swiftness and
the summer vacation began to look entrancingly
near, not only to Richard, but to Louise and Asbury as well.

One day, perhaps a month before commencement, Louise and Emma had gone to their room
from a rehearsal of some music for commencement, when Emma, who had been balancing herself upon the edge of the bed, said, " Louise, I tell
you you have a fortune in your voice."

" A fortune!" and Louise's lips curled a bit at the
thought. " And so, Miss Thrifty, I suppose I had
better go on the stage."

"Oh, you need not be so uppish about the matter,"
Emma replied, with schoolgirl freedom. " There
might be a fortune and still no stage. Our church
pays Mrs. Stanton twenty-five dollars each Sabbath,
which is a fortune not to be sneered at, with no
stage to bother a conscientious little Puritan."

" Twenty-five dollars for a few songs," mused
Louise when alone. " Twenty-five dollars Sabbath after Sabbath, even for a few months. How
many comforts such a sum would buy for the home
folks. Yes, how far such a sum would go towards
defraying the heavy college expenses." Louise
resolved in her heart to study even harder to bring
out every possible quality of her voice, and if—yes,
if the future should ever bring such an opportunity
she might be prepared to grasp it.

How strangely are the mingled threads of our
destiny interwoven. On the day following this
conversation Emma broke the seal of a letter from
home. Among other items of home news was the
casual one that Mrs. Stanton, the soprano, was in

rapidly failing health and had been ordered to the
mountains. The next mail home, unknown to
Louise, carried a letter extolling Louise's singing,
citing references if desired, and urging her father
to secure the position during the summer for Louise.
And strange to say (no not strange either, for
Emma's father was the one person in the church
who had this matter almost solely in charge, besides
he not only had great faith in his daughter's judgment but had grown to feel a great interest in the
sweet-voiced girl of whom she wrote so enthusias-
tically), a letter came offering the vacant place to
Louise for the summer, with the same salary as
that paid to Mrs. Stanton, with the added assurance
that if desired, a class of music pupils could be
secured. This seemed almost like an offer from a
fairyland to Louise. She wanted to accept it, but
then how hungry she had grown for the expected
visit home, and this would mean another year's
absence.

With realistic vividness the loved farmhouse arose
to view. There was father and mother, worn and
becoming bent with toil; then there were the boys,
pretty soon they ought to be knocking at a college
door; and there was Ruth and little Rose. Yes,
the family needs were imperative and certainly this
was a providential duty, and she must write the
home folks and get their sanction. And we too will
follow the letter bearing this question to its destination, the farm.

June with its rare wealth of beauty had come. The great rose climber which yearly changed the whole south side of the Stevenson home into a bewildering maze of beauty, hung full of great clusters of lovely roses.

Within the home Ruth and her mother were busy about the morning tasks. The great fireplace seems a bank of coolness, for Ruth with an artistic touch has filled it full of tall, fringe-like boughs of fullgrown asparagus, and upon the red bricks of the hearth stands a great old-fashioned bowl of roses. Just now she is placing another in the window ledge. As she does so she is saying to her mother, "I can hardly realize that within a very few weeks Asbury and Louise will be here. Dear me, how we will welcome them!" A tender smile played over the mother's lips as she replied, "and we must try not to think how few the weeks of the vacation will be."

Just then the sound of brisk hoofs echoed from the shady lane, and Edward soon came in, saying, "a letter from Louise!"

Mrs. Stevenson sat down to read, and read with growing wonder the offer of the distant church. Father soon came in, and together the wonderful news was discussed. "No, they could not consider the offer." Give up Louise for another year! But an hour ago life had seemed richer, fuller, as the memory of the sweet girl had brightened the little room. So said Rachel, so thought the father,

and so said the brothers and sisters. Rachel took
the letter to again read, in the quiet of the little
back porch. What a tempting offer it was, after
all. Just then her eyes lighted upon her husband
who, lost in thought, had leaned half wearily
against the well curb. Yes, he was growing old,
if not in years, at least in toil. How bent the
form! The plain working garb gave no hint of
the strong, honest heart which throbbed underneath
this uncouth covering. A sense of the superior advantages the children were having swept through
her heart, then she turned again to a paragraph in
Louise's letter.

"At first I could not think of this, I want so
much to see you all, but when I remember how
hard you all work, and how soon the other children will demand an education, I am forced to believe this offer is a Providence and that I ought to
go."

Rachel was glad the inexorable dinner claimed
her attention, that she might rid herself in action of
this new question that clamored for a settlement.
And it was settled. Another day a letter went to
Louise, bidding her God speed, and saying perhaps it was best that she should go.

Emma, in true school girl fashion, almost went
wild over the decision, for it had been her greatest
wish that Louise should accompany her home, and
now it was coming about as she had wished. And
she gave expression to her delight by waltzing the

highly perturbed Louise about the room in the most approved school girl fashion.

Asbury had known nothing of all this, as yet. On the very day this home letter had come to Louise, Emma met him on the college walk (by the way, we have not had time to mention it before, these young people were getting to be extraordinarily good friends,) and forthwith proceeded to tell him the wonderful piece of news. He of course was more than surprised, and with the surprise was mingled a queer feeling he could not define. He knew it was a trial for Louise to give up her visit home, a trial to the home folks to give it up; still it was such rare good luck, why wasn't there anything he could do? But no, his duty seemed plain, he must go home and help through the summer on the farm.

Louise dreaded most of all to tell Richard, for they had counted so much on the Summer together, but while she hesitated a letter came from him, telling her his father wanted him to take a western trip as soon as vacation had come, and look after some land, which would take perhaps a month or longer, but that on his way home he would stop for a visit. Poor Louise; she must not be thought lacking in loyalty to the home folks if after this letter there came a greater reconciliation to the loss of her vacation. These few remaining weeks were given to hard study, for she determined to

9

make herself worthy of Emma's strong commendation.

One day as she was returning from practice Emma came rushing out to meet her, saying a stranger had called, and before she had time to think she was ushered into the presence of Richard Newton, who having finished the year's examinations, and caring nothing for the closing exercises, had come on again to be in the presence of her whom he had so truly loved. Ah, the all sufficiency of those hours! The skies seemed bluer and brighter than ever before, the lazy flecks of white clouds floated above in a dreamy sort of way, strangely indicative of the present completeness of the life of each. Let heartaches cease, let forebodings for the future be still, simply to be together was happiness enough in itself. Richard found that the shy country girl he had loved and won had in a year become such a perfect woman that any man might feel proud, even of a glance. Hard study and cultured surroundings had done their work well in rounding and developing the person as well as the mind.

But his greatest surprise came when he heard her sing. Yes, that was the same old sweet voice which had joined with him in many a duet in that far off time, their childhood, or in the later years of their academy life, but how changed. Had he ever dreamed of anything so full and rich, and with a thrill of pride he said over and over to himself, "and she is mine; that true heart is mine forever."

The wealth of Crœsus is none too great to lay at the feet of such a peerless creature! How annoying the fate that had brought his father to such financial straits! Oh well, he had tided through a year, perhaps in another, his feet would be on firm ground again. If not, this woman he loved would value wealth of mind and of heart higher than of purse, and nothing should deter or hinder him in climbing the highest intellectual heights.

Such were his thoughts, such his meditations, but why just here did he pause, or why the sudden mantling of his cheek? Oh, for the world he would not have Louise know of the coarseness of the Braceton set, and most of all would he keep from her the fact that slowly but most surely had influences been at work till now he was an accredited member of the Braceton set. How he despised himself and his weakness as he remembered the wild, hilarious evenings, when with wine and cards he and the fellows had had a "time." Looking now into Louise's clear eyes he saw the danger, for he had through the collegiate year often argued to himself, "why should I not belong to their crowd? They all come from families that represent wealth and culture; besides they are all good fellows, and mean nothing more than the enlivenment of the dull routine of college life." What if there were wine and cards? He did not expect to become a total abstainer; even now in his father's cellar were bottles of choice, rich home-made wines, and as for cards? Yes, there *were* people strangely prejudiced against them but the shapely white hands of his mother had first taught him skill in their use. Of course with all this, as she had said, "discretion" must be used, and he prided himself upon the possession of this valuable quality.

Yet, would he have had Louise know this "discretion" had more than once failed him during these closing weeks, and that he had been taken to his room the worse for wine?

When he had first gone to college the Sabbath bells awakened thoughts of Louise and of God. He had gone regularly then to church, for while there in some way he had seemed nearer her, but with the flight of the months and under the influence of his new companions he had gone less and less. Yet now, looking into the pure eyes of Louise, he was conscious of a desire for a different life. What if after all the Stevenson theory of life was the correct one, what if Aunt Rachel were not a fanatic. He had so often heard her called that.

Yet he could not allow such uncomfortable thoughts to mar this week of great happiness, so he resolutely brushed aside the obtruding thought. There was the usual crowding into one little week sermons, lectures and addresses. To all such it became his pleasure to accompany his betrothed.

One evening there was a lecture before one of the ladies' literary societies. The subject of the

speaker was the old one of a "Woman's Kingdom," which after a few complimentary prefa-
tory remarks concerning women as philanthro-
pists, reformers, et al., he proceeded to show
was the home. One sentence burned into the
brain of Richard Newton. It was this:

"There can be no such a thing as happiness
when husband and wife find themselves with uncongenial tastes. The home is a superstructure
depending for its success upon the complete union
of two hearts, and this union cannot exist between
persons of tastes diametrically opposed."

"Oh, that is all nonsense!" Richard had said to
himself as the speaker urged caution upon a young
girl of religious habits who found herself coming
to care for a man who did not.

Still in his heart he paid the compliment to the
speaker by resolving to eschew the friendship of
the Braceton set.

CHAPTER XIII.

THE PREACHER—A SOPRANO—FLOSSIE.

THE week passed all too quickly; soon Asbury and Richard had turned their faces toward the home of their childhood, and Louise was journeying eastward in her new capacity of wage earner.

Asbury received a warm welcome home, though the joy, like many another joy, had its bitter edge, for the bright young girl, who should have accompanied him was miles away, and many months must elapse before she would brighten the home with her presence.

He showed at once how utterly unspoiled he was by going to work on the farm with all the energy of his nature, spurred on it must be confessed, by the secret thought that work hard as he might, dainty girlish Louise was doing more than he.

What a comfort he was to his father, and how he grew to lean upon him and to place more and more upon those broad, manly shoulders the burdens of the farm. As for Rachel, never did Hannah in the sweet old Bible story, feel more genuine mother pride in her priestly son than did this modern mother in this her first-born, chosen of the Lord.

His influence too was felt outside the home circle, for he became a wonderful inspiration to the young people of the church. Indeed it has never been estimated how much good one intelligent, thoroughly consecrated young man can do in influencing and holding to the right other young people of less well established principles.

During the summer an event occurred which throughout his whole life served to bind him to the home church. That is, he was licensed to preach. It occurred in this wise: at a meeting of the church officiary, the pastor had presented his name, and the necessary papers were prepared which gave him an accredited right to preach the gospel, his mother knowing nothing at the time of the intention.

When his father returned from this meeting he went at once to the kitchen where she was at work, and thinking to surprise her said, " Mother, you must have a little extra for dinner; the preacher will dine with us." And she taking the matter seriously, indeed knowing no reason why she should not, replied, scarcely looking up, " Well, catch me one of those plump chickens out at the barn." Willing to humor the joke John went out to the barn and soon a chicken lay quivering in a vessel on the table. Leaving the dressing

to Ruth Rachel slipped on a fresh apron and went
in for a word of greeting with the guest. Greatly
to her surprise no one was about.

"They have gone out on the farm to discuss the
growing crops and stock." So saying to herself
she went out to the kitchen and soon an appetizing
dinner was spread. In response to the dinner call
her husband, with Asbury and the rest of the family promptly presented themselves.

"Why, where is the preacher?" asked Rachel,
looking about.

"Here," and John Stevenson laid his sunbrowned
hand upon the broad shoulders of his first-born.

Happy mother! Though for more than a year
she had known this was to be, yet the announcement of the finality thrilled her unaccountably.
He was near her when his father bore the news,
and she bent forward with a kiss, saying, "Having
put your hands to the plough, see to it that with
you there shall be no turning back."

The words seemed prophetic. Years after when
the way was especially rough the remembrance of
this home scene, and his mother's words held him
closely to his work.

*   *   *   *   *

Richard Newton found little to interest him with
Louise away. In a private talk with his father he
learned that the financial outlook had not improved,
and that unless something unforseen should occur,
the inevitable must soon be faced. Mr. Newton, a

victim of that strange cowardice that often affects
men of his stamp, had found it impossible to acquaint his family with the threatened disaster, and
Richard knowing it all, looked with a bitterness
akin to anger upon the luxuries on every side.

Upon his return he found preparations were
being made on a lavish scale for Marie's wedding,
which was to occur in the early July, to allow of a
western and mountain tour.

Her betrothed held a good position in his father's
bank, and there was no reason why the wedding
should be longer delayed. So at the appointed
time, amid a great deal of eclat, Marie went out
from her father's home.

The Stevensons were among the invited guests,
but only Asbury and Ruth were present. These
returned with glowing accounts of the elegance of
the lunch, the richness of the bride's trousseau and
the value of the presents, among the last being a
deed from Mr. Newton for one of the handsomest
residences in the town, which was to be the bride's
future home.

After the departure of the bridal party Richard
too took a western train, carefully instructed by his
father, who assured him that upon the value
of some western investments depended freedom from disaster. But before he went a long
letter bore to Louise an account of the wedding,
and assurance of his undying love.

* * * * *

In a large city not far from the steady plash of ocean's wave, on a lovely June Sabbath, a young girl awaited with a beating heart the hour for service in the great aristocratic stone church, which faced one of the loveliest avenues in that great city. One does not need to be told that this is our young friend Louise. She had known before coming that Emma's home was one of luxury, and that the church in which she was to sing was one of the best in the city, yet country raised as she had been, she had not dreamed of such magnificence. The rich mellow light stole in and was filtered through the translucent mosaic of the windows. The very echo of her foot fall as she had glided up the aisle had been caught and held imprisoned in the soft, yielding plush of the carpet. The pews, indeed every appointment of the church, betokened luxury and wealth.

Could she hope to satisfy so critical an audience as worshipped there?

Emma was sure that she could, yet Louise had never in her life been self-confident, and it was little wonder that she trembled in anticipation of the ordeal.

She had taken her place early, and as the audience gathered she saw more than one curious glance towards the new soprano. The great organ pealed forth its most sonorous melody, then died away into a gentle accompaniment. She was about to sing. The book she held was open at that

matchless solo, "I know that my Redeemer Liveth."
With the first note of the organ had gone up a
whispered prayer. For answer came with wonderful distinctness, a vision of home and the sweet
home faith of her parents, and of the plain
home church where she had knelt and received
knowledge of sins forgiven. Ah, yes, she knew of
a truth what she was about to sing, and without a
falter the clear young voice took up the refrain and
bore it aloft and sang it so feelingly that the audience, with a first gesture of surprise, settled itself
to simple enjoyment. She had won!

As she sat down the tremulous plume on Mrs.
De Manderville's bonnet nodded by far too vigor-
ously to suit the usual calm poise of that lady, as she
whispered to Mrs. Millionaire just at elbow touch
with her, "A wonderful voice; yes, a wonderful
voice."

"Yes, and a wonderful amount of *heart*, too," Mrs.
Millionaire had telegraphed back, and if any one
had a right to recognize this last named quality,
certainly it was this same lady for a great many of
the poor of her city and the interests of her church
accused her of a like possession, and blessed the
thousands that accompanied it.

Louise had expected on coming that with Emma's
or her mother's help she would secure a good boarding house, but both Mr. and Mrs. Ward would allow no such thing. Their house was large and
roomy, they said, and to allow Emma's friend to

seek a home elsewhere could not be thought of. So throughout all the long delightsome days of that summer Louise was an inmate of this luxurious home. For the first time in her life she came to know the meaning of the word "leisure," but her industrious soul could not brook the enforced idleness. So she talked with Mrs. Ward about securing a class of music pupils. Now the Wards, though among the most wealthy and cultured of the great congregation which gathered in the aristocratic stone church, and with a little touch of perhaps excusable pride, could look back on several generations of ancestors possessing like qualities, yet no dwellers in cottage or country farm were ever more sensible, nor held more exalted notions of the true dignity of labor, and instead of discouraging Louise rejoiced in her disposition to work. Mrs. Ward went at once to Mrs. Millionaire about the matter, and very soon Louise had a good paying class.

Nor did this young Christian fail to identify herself with the active work of the church. She found that this particular church, luxurious though it was, undertook and carried on much practical Christian work. Under the especial fostering care of Mrs. Millionaire was a band of young girls who even so many years ago as that, made for their special object the study of the great work of foreign missions and the raising of funds for the same. Into this Louise entered with all her heart. Years ago her interest had been awakened by letters from the girl wife of a missionary. With such a foundation she developed such an intelligent interest that Mrs. Millionaire learned to depend more and more upon her. A passing glance at this lady may not be out of place.

Though her purse and bank account were alike heavy, yet her real wealth lay in her active, clear brain, her philanthropic nature, and her true consecration to her Master's cause. She had been for years (this was before the era of separate missionary organizations in each denomination) a valued manager in the Woman's Union Missionary Society, and of her great wealth she held herself to be but a steward. She felt that her best brain work must be done in using this for the advancement of Christ's kingdom, and was never happier than when she found a young enthusiastic person who evinced an interest in these matters that lay so near her heart. Little wonder she seized upon and grew to love the bright-faced, earnest young soprano.

Thus the summer passed happily. Her singing gave great satisfaction and her class of music pupils gave her full employment.

The Ward family consisted of a younger brother and sister besides a married daughter, Mrs. Herron, the mother of two sweet little children, who with their mother were often at their grandfather's house.

From Emma she learned that Mr. Herron was a lawyer, his father Judge Herron being one of the most highly and favorably known men in the state.

The young pair had a lovely home on one of the boulevards, but in an indefinable and intangible way Louise found that there was something wrong, what, she could not tell, for there would come days when the young wife would stay at her father's house, remaining most of the time in her room, and if seen, her eyes would be red with weeping.

One day as Emma was driving her about the city, upon one of the fashionable streets the eye of Louise was caught by a large and beautiful building.

Upon inquiring the use, or name of the structure, Emma responded with more bitterness than Louise had ever seen her manifest, " The Devil's gateway."

" Why, what do you mean?"

" Just what I say. It is a fashionable club house, and there Tom Herron imbibes the demon that is killing my sister. Yes, I believe it will kill her!"

Louise was silent. Could young Herron be a common drunkard?

Emma continued: "Oh, I hate it. I hate it, hate it! I hate everything that wine touches. I would as soon marry an Asiatic leper as a man who takes a single glass."

Why did Louise start? Why did her heart sink so suddenly? Ah, but Richard, it was all false, he had never drank; she would lay down her life on that certainty. Still the vehement words of Emma rankled in her heart.

This question had always seemed so far off, so remote, so associated with people in another world from her own. She thought of her good father, of her brothers, and rejoiced that they were safe, but could it be possible that this serpent could wind its sinuous way into a Christian home as it surely had into the Ward's?

Perhaps a month passed and the shadows seemed almost gone from pretty Mrs. Herron's face, when one night Louise was awakened by a noise at the street door.

"Oh, let me in, do let me in, quick!"

"It is Lucy's voice," said Emma, springing up to go to the door. Her father was before her, and in a moment the trembling, weeping woman entered, herself half clad, and with sweet baby Flossie in her arms and Master Harry, these two in their night clothes as she had snatched them from their cot and fled.

There was no attempt now to hide the family skeleton. Lucy told them that for weeks, as indeed they had known, her husband had been sober and repentant. As usual he had made many promises of reform, but oh, the dreadful appetite; how like a caged wild beast! "An hour ago," she continued, "he came home wild, beside himself with frenzy, threatening to kill both himself and me, and oh, I was sure he would," (at another time he would have lain down his life for this woman,) "when I fled through the door with the children."

Just then there was a scramble at the **door.** Louise drew back in horror as a wild-eyed reeling **man entered. Could this** be the elegant Mr. Herron, **usually the marvel** of good breeding? Yes, having **missed his wife and dimly** realizing in his **frenzy that** she must have gone **to her** father's, he **had in** his drunken fury followed her. Before any **one** could know or guess his design, indeed, it all occurred in less time that it has taken to record it, **he** wildly **fired at** his **wife, who** upon his entrance **had** stood **with Flossie in her arms,** then placing **the muzzle to his own heart,** fired, and fell forward dead.

Mrs. Herron, too, lay upon the **floor, but** whether killed or not, not **one knew in that awful** hour. Emma was the only one who retained her self-possession, and she stooped to take from the **arms so tightly** clasping her little Flossie, when she **suddenly cried** out:

"God help us, Flossie is **killed!**"

It was true. The bullet intended for his wife **had in an instant** stilled the infant life, but the mother was unhurt. Her's was the harder fate, to awaken to a knowledge of what had occurred. Words cannot picture the woe and desolation of that hour.

Soon the bleeding body **of** the self-murdered man was borne to the home of his father, but a few blocks away. The young wife and mother, in a darkened room, moaned in the wildest delirium, and sweet baby Flossie lay a mute sacrifice upon the altar of strong drink.

Later, as Louise, with a heartache she had never before known, sang the sad chant over the little murdered victim, she said down in her heart, "Yes, Emma is right; I too hate it, hate it, hate it! I will have nothing to do in all my life with any one at all connected with this horrible evil."

Ah, Louise, it is well for you that mother nature gave you from out her rich storehouse, a will so strong that had you lived in an earlier day you could have stood unflinchingly, if duty so demanded, amid the pile of lighted fagots, else in the heavy ordeal of the future you had not been able to abide by those words.

When Louise had gone for the summer to Emma's home, it was with the confident expectation of spending the last two weeks at home, but in the coming of the sudden catastrophe new qualities of heart were developed. The stricken family came in after years to look back upon those dreadful days and say, "How could we have lived if it had not been for Louise?"

She had that rare faculty that instinctively sees the right thing to do, yet her helpfulness was not that obtrusive, bustling kind which annoys while it helps, but in her gentleness she it

10

was who could best soothe, and to Mrs. Ward she
came to be a tower of strength.

Poor Mrs. Herron lay for days in delirium and
then settled down into a stony, tearless apathy from
which nothing would arouse her.   Her friends
feared insanity.

One day as Louise sat in the music room she saw
her glide down into the room beyond and throw
herself upon the spot where little Flossie's coffin
had stood.   Her attitude betokened extreme and
hopeless dejection.

" Shall I do it? " whispered Louise to herself.

" I can but try," and seating herself at the piano
her clear rich voice rang out:

> " Rock of Ages, cleft for me
>   Let me hide myself in thee."

Tenderly came the words:

> " Leave, oh leave me not alone,
>   Still support and comfort me."

Could it be possible?   Yes, the heartbroken
woman was sobbing.

In an instant Louise was with her pouring forth
words of comfort, and gradually she was won back
to an interest in life, by the sweet power of Christian song.

*   *   *   *   *

It was with sorrowing hearts that Mr. and Mrs.
Ward watched the train as in the early September
it bore Louise and Emma back to school.

They arrived a few hours before the train which

was to bring Asbury. How vividly Louise recalled the time when, a year ago, she had come as a stranger; now it seemed everybody knew her. Grave seniors called out "All hail!" Professors gave warm greetings, and in the gladness of her welcome the pangs of homesickness that she had felt at not being able to see the home-folks melted away. And then came Asbury, big brown Asbury, fresh from the farm. Louise thought he had never looked so handsome, he of the broad shoulders, and countenance as free from guile as her own.

Then there were the innumerable questions to be asked.

"Yes, father and mother are well. Father not very strong, though."

Ruth? She and Edward have gone back to the Academy. Ruth was taller than her mother, and Edward was almost as tall as his father, and as fond of books as ever. Yes, the new house would be finished in a short time.

Oh, yes; Marie and her husband had just gotten back and settled down to elegant housekeeping.

Therese had a French music teacher who squinted, wore glasses, and rumor said made love to his pupils, Therese in particular.

Mr. Newton was said to be growing richer; some western speculations had proven especially good. "But I would rather have our own father and mother," said Asbury, "rich as they are in their good qualities, than the wealth of a nabob."

All this and more Asbury poured into the ears of his sister.

She had yet one surprise before settling down to study and that was the sudden arrival of Richard, who decided to stop on his way back to his college.

How full of joy the hours were. How full of plans for the future.

Richard hoped in another year to be able to claim his bride, so each went to their year's work full of hope and of good cheer.

CHAPTER XIV.

THERESE—BANKRUPTCY.

LEAVING the students to become adjusted to another year's work, we again turn to the home life of the two families. Some of the news so briefly epitomized by Asbury deserves more than passing mention. The year on the farm had been reasonably successful, and while the collegiate course abroad and the academic one at home had entailed extra expense above what each had deposited from his or her "college fund," yet the growing family made such an imperative demand for more room that Rachel and Ruth saw with extreme satisfaction the lumber arrive that represented two good front rooms, one with a bay window for Ruth's flowers, and two greatly needed sunny bedrooms, and in a few days the welcome noise of saws and hammers broke the stillness of the country air.

Ruth and Edward were again in the Academy. Ruth was now, as Asbury had said, taller than her mother; it seemed startling how she had shot up to womanhood. From her earliest childhood she

had been of a quiet and loving disposition.
The busy, hardworking life the Stevensons led had
a tendency in itself to throw each child on its own
resources, and particularly the care of the younger
children upon the older.   Was a little brain puzzled
over a lesson?   None so patient, so ready to help
as Ruth; indeed none so capable, for she had the
gift of making another' understand whatever was
plain to her own mind.   Since Louise and Asbury had
gone she had become the family reader, and many an
evening was made enjoyable as her low, well modulated voice read from the current literature in
which the family were interested, for though the old
house had remained small the library had grown
with the family, until now it was of really respectable dimensions and each book showed
marks of frequent reading.   There was one work
in the collection which marked an epoch in the
life of Edward, who the family laughingly insisted had gone mad on botany.   It all began in a
little paragraph which had caught his eye in the
early spring, which in an entertaining way told its
young readers the pleasures of seed knowledge,
suggesting that some seeds be placed to soak and
the result watched.   Edward followed the suggestion, and for a time the various cups and saucers
that sat around holding sprouting seeds were a
trial to his mother and Ruth.   From this simple
beginning he had become really well versed in the
subject of plant life.

There was also a volume on mineralogy which had guided in the gathering of quite a valuable collection of geological specimens.

Fiction was not wholly lacking in this home library, but this was selected with the greatest care and from the best authors. It was held to have a proper place in the family, perhaps in the ratio of sweetmeats to the staples of the table.

Perhaps the reader asks, "How did this plain, hard working man and woman come to have such good taste and judgment in literature and the children such fondness for it?" Does it seem unreasonable? Rachel herself would have told you that beginning with those first quiet evenings when she and her young husband had read together by the blazing fire their taste had grown naturally, and that the eccentric (?) friend of the camp ground had builded far better than even he knew.

A feature of their year's reading had been a weekly review of the best books published, so they were kept informed as to what the great world of thought was doing. Moreover, the undercurrent of this reading from it had been a quiet sermon for higher education, and they had been led to plan for their children's wider education, and with that education came the natural introduction to the broad field of science and literature.

Before we turn to others who are beginning to urge their claims, we must speak of Edward. He was like, and yet unlike Asbury. There never had

been a time when it was not the latter's delight to
throw aside his book and help his father in harvesting a load of hay or reaping a field of wheat, but it
early became evident that Edward had no such desires.   He did his tasks conscientiously, but there
was no pleasure to him in the work.

When a task was given him he hurriedly finished
it to get off with a book, and in some quiet spot,
perhaps the hay mow, he would lie for hours obliv-
ious of everything else.   In this way he followed
the conquering Alexander around the world and
read of the triumphs of Cyrus.   How he revelled
in Irving's "Conquest of Granada," dreaming by
day if not by night of old Moorish castles and
buried treasures, or became a living companion
of Rip Van Winkle and Ichabod Crane.

John often asked Rachel what they would do
with the farm, when the boys seemed to care more
for books than ploughing.   "But *you* will be father's right hand man," he would wind up by saying,
as he laid his hand on the sunburnt, honest face of
the young John, who now proudly made a "hand"
by the side of his father.

* * * * *

"Mother," said Ruth one day, when upon her
return from school she had donned a work apron
and was helping about the evening meal, "I do
believe Therese is actually in love with Monsieur
Les Page, the French music master."

"Impossible!" replied the mother, "she knows

nothing of him, besides he is old, old enough for her father."

"Well, all that may be true, but she talks of him constantly, writes him letters, and I believe"— Here Ruth paused.

"What is it?" asked Rachel.

"Well, I ought not to tell, perhaps, but a week ago she came from her music lesson in the music room all flustrated and she showed me a little pink note, heavily scented and said triumphantly, 'Edith Lancaster thinks monsieur is so devoted to her. See here! what would she say if she knew of this,' and she showed me the note signed by the professor."

"I tell you what it is, mother," continued Ruth, "Therese lives in a world of fiction; she is constantly imagining herself a heroine in some startling drama—you know she just feeds on novels."

A shade of questioning anxiety crossed Mrs. Stevenson's face.

"No, she said softly, I wouldn't dare." A momentary remembrance of the old Lynton days had arisen in her mind.

Should she warn Margaret? No! She had chosen her line of action in regard to her family as Rachel had hers.

The next morning Ruth and Edward started, as was their custom, for the Academy. An hour later Rachel caught sight of Ruth. She ran out, exclaiming, "Edward! Edward! is he hurt?"

"No."

"Therese! Oh mother! Monsieur Les Page and Therese have gone."

"Oh! if it were my child! Poor Margaret! But I dare not go to her," Rachel said to herself. Soon she had learned all there was to tell.

Therese had gone the evening before, ostensibly to spend the night with a friend. Not returning the next morning her mother thought she had gone to school so was not alarmed. But when monsieur's absence was also noted, and some said he had boarded the midnight train with a lady, heavily veiled, rumor became rampant.

Still, Mrs. Newton never dreamed of connecting the veiled lady with her daughter, till going by chance to Therese's room she found it in disorder and many articles gone.

Sending hurriedly to the friend's home where she was to visit over night, she learned to her dismay that she had left there between nine and ten o'clock.

Yes, it was true! Out from a home of wealth this child of luxury, hardly yet in the dawn of womanhood, had flown with this unknown adventurer who had proven his baseness by using his position to win the love of a foolish, romantic girl, rather not that he cared for her love, but rather to gain access to the reputed great wealth of the Newtons.

To attempt to portray the agonized sorrow of Margaret in those days would be useless, with her old-time characteristics, she closed her shutters, shut out the sunlight and friends and bore her sorrow alone.

Writing Richard he could do nothing, and to remain where he was, Mr. Newton telegraphed in every direction, employed detectives, but it was many long weeks before the pair were located in that great human ocean, New York City.

Hither Monsieur Les Page had brought the girl with promises of love and protection, and here for a time we must leave them, though Mr. Newton tried by every possible means to get his daughter to return.

Therese wrote of their marriage a theatrically glowing letter, as one of her heroines might, of her great happiness, lauded to the skies "love in a cottage" (poor child, it was only a fourth rate boarding house, but then cottage sounded better), and closed with the modest request that her father would allow her her patrimony, the latter a sugges- tion of the Monsieur.

Cause enough for sorrow this, but it lacked much of being the only cause Mr. Newton had in those days for anxiety. From the earliest pages of this history the business ability of this man has been praised, but for years not content with the slow gains of the mill, he had speculated, now in west- ern, now in eastern stocks, now he became a large stockholder in a western railroad, or in a mine whose output promised fabulous returns. Of course much of this speculation was done on borrowed capital. This was all right as long as the returns were all right.

But there came a change. Stocks that he had expected to rise, suddenly fell and kept falling, involving losses of thousands of dollars. Try hard as he might to keep his business interests from the prying world, yet undefined and ugly rumors had been current for more than a year.

The western investments Richard had gone to look after the last summer had proven good, and he contrived to have a local notice in the papers chronicling the large gains in that direction, but these proved nearly valueless in adjusting matters. For months past the toils had been tightening about him; promising ventures melted into thin air.

It was true the actual business of the mill was still profitable, but these profits in comparison with the liabilities were as nothing, so that in just three months from the time Therese fled he wrote Richard as follows:

" In another week all will be over, and the world will know me as a bankrupt. God knows I have tried to avert it, and tried in vain. I am truly sorry for the heartache it will cause others.

"I have secured the returns from the western stocks you invested in last summer, and I trust these will be sufficient to enable you to complete the course of study you have begun.

"I am thankful I secured a home for Marie. She

is comfortable and will know no difference in her life.

"Years ago when this trouble first threatened, I secured the home to your mother, and indeed it was really hers from her father, so we will not be homeless.

"You will see now, more than ever, how necessary it is for you to arm yourself with an education and a profession.

"When the blow falls do not come home.

FATHER."

A week later there was an account in the great city papers of the failure of William Newton, of Burton, owner of great milling interests.

But few of the readers cared; men were constantly failing. Yes, a mere episode.

The local papers of Burton took up the matter more thoroughly. His enterprise as a citizen was enlarged upon, regrets were profuse that such a calamity should have fallen upon him. Satisfaction was expressed that the beautiful home, long a center of hospitality, had been for years the private property of Mrs. Newton. The rest of the property Mr. Newton had honorably placed in the hands of his creditors.

Mr. Newton, after the news had become public and the first stab of disgrace was past, experienced a feeling of relief. The effects of a blow are often easier to be borne than the dread, and if it had not been for the erring Therese and two other facts

William Newton might have been happier than
he had been for years.

One of these was that his wife had sunk beneath
the blow. It had come upon her suddenly, and following her daughter's ill assorted marriage it had
proven more than she could bear. In a heavily
curtained upper chamber she was fighting the battle of life and death.

The other reason? Ah! when it obtruded itself
into the sick room or followed the sorrowing man
to his couch (and when during the past years had
it not?) involuntarily he cast his eyes in the direction of the farmhouse, where this very night he
knew a peaceful family had gathered, with no other
feeling in their hearts than generous compassion for
the misfortunes of an old time friend and neighbor.

Read on, sweet voiced Ruth! Unconsciously to
you, you are the central figure in a sweet home
group. Father sits contentedly in his easy chair;
the knitting in mother's hands does not hinder the
close attention she always gives when you read.
The brothers are grouped near the plain old table.
Read on; it will be many a day before this same
group will gather so contentedly again.

CHAPTER XV.

JOHN, THE YOUNGER.

T WAS a blustering wintry day. A heavy snow had lain for weeks on the ground, then had come a warm wind, a few days of sunshine and it had melted, save a few patches on the hill-sides. This had been followed by another freeze, and now this morning the winter wind blew across the empty meadows and whistled noisily about the farm house.

Ruth and Edward were each at the Academy; Rose was at the country school. John, the young prototype of his father, had begged to remain at home, asserting that Madam Blanch, a portly Berkshire dame, needed his assistance in moving her large family of baby Berkshires into better quarters.

After the morning chores Rachel went, where she was soon joined by her husband, to look over again those wonderful rooms now ready for occupancy, and into which they expected to move next week.

"How Louise will love this sunny room," Rachel was saying, "she can share it with Ruth, and if she brings her friend Miss Ward home with her, we can at least make her comfortable."

"Dear me! How sad was that terrible tragedy in her home."

"Yes," replied her husband, who was with her, "and think of Newton. We have so much to be thankful for in that sorrow has never yet knocked at our door."

Ah! but dear hearts have ye not read

> "Into the life of each some rain must fall;
> Some days must be dark and dreary?"

Care such as you have never known is already close at hand.

Just then Rachel passed the window. "Why, father! who are those strangers near the barn?"

"Looking out John saw two men walking leisurely about, taking a careful survey of the premises and belongings.

"Probably some men looking for stock. I'll walk out and meet them."

So saying he took his hat and started to meet the strangers, and Rachel being left alone busied herself about the dinner.

But the strangers, whoever they were, seemed to have no business with Mr. Stevenson, for by the time he reached the barn, they were letting down the pasture bars and going toward the woodland beyond.

"Father," said younger John impetuously, as they surrounded the dinner table, "who were those two men who were walking over the farm this morning, acting as if they owned it?"

"I am sorry I can't tell you," responded his father, "I supposed they were stock men and went out to see them, but they had gone over toward the woods."

"Well, they came along where I was at work penning up Madam Blanche and asked me a lot of questions they had no business to. I guess they didn't get much out of me."

"I hope you remembered to be polite," interposed his mother.

"I guess I was polite enough, but when the thin chap with spectacles asked me if there was any mortgage on the place I told him no, and if there was I guessed we could pay it."

Ruth and her mother were yet busied with the after dinner work, when there came a knock at the door, and from the kitchen Rachel could see the visitors were none other than the two strangers of the morning.

A forboding of evil, she scarcely knew what, seized her, and both she and Ruth hastened that they might know the import of the strangers' visit.

No need, for in a few minutes her husband, white and trembling, appeared at the door and required her presence. Ruth mutely followed.

"Mother," said John Stevenson, with unconscious, rugged dignity, "this gentleman," indicating a florid, rather large man evidently ill at ease, "is Mr.

11

Hardin, one of Mr. Newton's creditors. This,"
indicating evidently the 'thin chap with spectacles,'
is his lawyer, Mr. Nevins."

"Did you not years ago take my message to
William Newton that I could not longer remain as
security with him on the note?"   "Certainly,"
replied Rachel, "he consented to the change and
assured me the name would be removed at once."

The lawyer took from his pocket a leather book
and from its folds took out a yellow bit of paper.
With a blur over his eyes John Stevenson read the
fateful words:

"I promise to pay the sum of ten thousand dollars with interest from date," etc. Signed. There
was the pen flourish of Mr. Newton, and the unmis-
takable, cramped, plain "John Stevenson," and the
flourished William Newton was as worthless as the
yellow paper on which it was written!

A moment of choking stillness followed. The
old clock on the high wooden mantel ticked on
loudly and bravely, as if it would fain avert the
coming disaster.

The hickory fire that glowed in the great fireplace snapped and sputtered, but the living actors
in this home tragedy stood or sat like figures of
carved marble.

John Stevenson looked in mute appeal into the
faces of the two men, both of whom were fidgeting
and moving around in an uneasy manner, but there

was no pity, no relenting. They were there to have their "pound of flesh."

"There must be some awful mistake," almost gasped Rachel, "certainly William Newton could not be guilty of this awful crime."

Ruth with clenched hands was crying piteously as she leaned with one arm over her father's chair. Edward stood in silent wonder, but no one had noticed the fiery young John who suddenly sprang to his feet, and with eyes blazing like coals and a face with the pallor of death, save for the rugged tan, placed himself in front of his father and said:

"Father, what does all this mean? What right have these men," and boy as he was they were forced to wince at the scorn in his voice—"to come here and annoy you?"

"It means, my son," and the father's voice seemed as if the heartache of a life-time was crowded into a second, "that years ago, for old friendship's sake, I became security to William Newton for a sum of money which, with the interest, will take every foot of ground belonging to the farm to pay. He assured me at the time he would only need my signature for a year, and afterwards gave me to understand that it was paid."

"Oh! the scoundrel! but it isn't right, it isn't just. Think how they have lived while we have worked hard day after day."

"Go!" and he turned in youthful fury to the

two men, and flung wide open the outside door.
"Let the Newtons pay their own debts."

The men arose to leave, glad to escape from an interview so embarassing, preferring to leave their cause to the surer officers of the law.

Both the father and mother were so overwhelmed with this calamity that they scarcely realized John's brusque speech, and were only too glad to be left alone.

Long they sat and talked, but talking brought little relief, only serving to emphasize the direful fact more plainly that William Newton had made a promise to Rachel which he had not fulfilled.

"Oh!" moaned Rachel, " if I only had not trusted him; had insisted on seeing for myself that the the note was paid as he said."

And now for this, her mistake, they were to be homeless. Carefully she recalled every incident of her call at the Newton office. Mr. Newton had told her again what she already knew, that " the money thus secured had been used as an investment in the rapidly changing financial scenes in the early days of the war; it had brought good returns and had been invested again and again." Yes, he had admitted it had been an act of business carelessness that the original note had not been paid. As she desired, it he " would write a check that very day."

And she had believed him. For herself she did not care so much, but there were the years of hardships born by her husband. He had never been strong since the hour of the accident. No, he could never make his way again.

The afternoon wore away, night came, though they retired, neither could sleep. There were the children! Rachel sobbed as she thought of them. It was true each had their own college fund; how she blessed the writer of the stray paragraph which had contained the suggestion, yet unless it was annually added to, it would prove insufficient. Would they finally have to give up and come home?

Following these sad reflections came the thought, "Asbury is the Lord's own. He will care for him someway."

Ah! if that is true of Asbury, why not of Louise, of Ruth, of each one. God's own are not all ministers. He will have his servants in all walks of life, and the first prayer that had crossed her lips now rose for sustaining grace to bear this trial if it came.

God is always waiting, longing to comfort if asked, and even as she prayed, peace came.

They were all the Lord's. He was pledged to care for them. The word, "I will never leave thee nor forsake thee," still stood, and David's experience as recorded, "Once was I young, now I am old, but I have never seen the righteous forsaken nor his seed begging bread," was comforting to her.

Reaching out her hand, ah! it had long been wrinkled and hard, she clasped the still browner one of her husband, and whispered, "John, be comforted. God reigns and He will care for us."

"Oh!" groaned John, "It was our own foolish act, and God cannot save us from the effects of such. We should not have allowed the years to pass without knowing that what he had promised was done."

"But God can, and will help us bear it," she urged, and so comforted, after a weary while they slept.

Before the old farm horn had blown the dinner summons the following day two things had happened. One was an interview on the part of John Stevenson with the man who had so cruelly wronged him, where he learned the truth of his worst fears. Yet he had come away with a queer feeling akin to pity for the wretched man, for he said to himself, "I can stand before the world an honest, if it must be, a penniless man, and there is a world of satisfaction in a clear conscience."

And it was true William Newton was an object of pity, for over and over again he had learned the gruesome, unwelcome lesson that the way of the transgressor is always hard. For months he had been cowering before the hour when the Stevenson's must know of his dishonesty.

At first he had not dreamed of a dishonest act. He had fully expected to cancel the note even

before Rachel's visit, and certainly to fulfill his
promise to her, but even then the web of entanglements had begun to enwrap him, and as fate would
have it, on the very day of her call, news reached
him of the sudden decline in price of grain, which
he had contracted for in large quantities. "Well,
the very next week I will do it," was the promise
he made his conscience when his last available
check was given, not to free the farm folk, but
other more clamorous creditors.

But affairs were no better "next week," and so
he had lived on, the note becoming the property of
a bank, whose managers were wise to recognize
the value of the plain, cramped signature. During
the last five years he had not entered upon a speculation without promising himself to redeem the
hated note with the margin, but it had been impossible. Thus often do the results of our actions
widely exceed our intentions.

During the interview he had sat cowed,
and shrunken Where was the old-time alertness,
the ready joke, the hearty good fellowship? Yes,
such are to be pitied "who sow to the wind, for of
the wind they shall reap destruction." Thinking
this, John Stevenson left him to his own sad
thoughts.

How misspent now seemed the years that had
been given solely to the getting of wealth. How
fatal the mistake that had made him merely a
"source of supply for his family." He groaned

aloud as thoughts of his children intruded. Could he hope, dare he hope, for Richard, handsome Richard! though possessing talents that ought to make him a leader among his fellows? He acknowledged now in those hours of bitterness that the whole bent of his boy's training had been such it would be nigh impossible for him to resist the temptations with which he was surrounded.

And Therese, blithe, headstrong Therese, there could be nothing but sorrow and failure in her life. And Marie? Perhaps here was a grain of comfort.

No! he frowned, who could feel pride in a vapid society woman, and to crown it all, up stairs lay the mother, his beautiful Margaret, tossing in delirium not yet conscious of the loss that had come to their old-time friends. We repeat he was to be pitied.

When John Stevenson arrived home after the interview he learned of the second event we have mentioned. A legal notice had been served demanding the immediate payment of the note and the interest from date.

Why go over the details of those trying days? Rachel's strength of character had never been tested till now. With her own hand she penned a letter bearing the terrible news to Asbury and Louise, telling them to remain at college for the present; that their presence at home would not help.

To her husband she became a tower of strength;

when he would have sunk she comforted him by reminding him that the family were well nigh grown, that somehow food and shelter and the equally pressing needs of an education would be supplied.

No one guessed the tempest that raged in the heart of sixteen year old John. Of all the children none loved the farm as he. While Asbury had dreamed of a pulpit, and Edward had followed a conquering hero around the world, John had found *his* study out under the blue sky. He knew every foot of ground and could give the name and history of each and every animal about the place. A flock of sheep ba-a-a-ed at the pasture bars each night; to each one he had given a name, and it had been with impatience he had listened to the statements "that all sheep looked alike." To give up the farm! and under such circumstances! With swelling heart he determined to see Mr. Newton himself. "Father's too easy," the children had often said.

Soon chance favored his purpose, for he was sent to Burton on an errand, and once there lost no time in making his way to the Newton residence. The angry blood surged through his veins as he trod the beautiful, well-kept lawn and beheld the elegant luxury of the home. A servant answered the bell, and went to call Mr. Newton. "No, he could not be seen."

"But tell him I *must* see him," said John.

Again word was brought back that he could not be seen.

"Where is he?" asked John.

"In his wife's room," replied the servant. John walked out as if leaving and the servant went back to her work.

He well knew each room of the great house, and little thinking of the sick one, he turned and sought the room where he knew Mr. Newton was. Soon his low knock summoned the surprised man to the door.

CHAPTER XVI.

A VISIT—A RESULT—LEAVING THE FARM.

"J HAD to see you," explained John, who swallowed back the involuntary pity which rose as he caught sight of the haggard man.

"It is a part of my punishment," the tired man said to himself, as he wearily led the way to a room where since his trouble he had kept some of his papers.

"Well," he said interrogatively, as the door closed behind them.

As the boy had gone about the farm yesterday and as he had ridden in this evening, he had longed to meet the author of their trouble face to face. How he would upbraid him. Ah! he had felt as if he only lacked opportunity to meet him, but as he beheld the pinched face, somehow the invectives died on his lips.

Yet a glance upon the elegant appointments of the room recalled him. "He ought to sell this, part with every comfort, for the debt was his." All this passed through his mind almost before the echo of the questioning "well" had died away.

"I came to ask," and the sunburned face of this boy, clad in his working clothes, shone with the righteousness of his request, "if you would do nothing to save my father and mother from being homeless, all for friendship to you?"

"I would gladly do it, if I could, but I cannot," and there was a hopeless ring in his voice.

"But it is so monstrous, so unjust," and the boy's face flushed at the thought. "Can you sit here in this home, with all this about you?" and he swept his hand to indicate the luxurious surroundings.

"Can you allow Marie to retain her home and see my father, now growing old, lose that for which he has worked through these long years, for you?"

Mr. Newton was silent, then said, "I cannot control Marie's home. Once I might; not now."

"But this home," persisted John, "you can easily sell it."

Said Mr. Newton, with a touch of impatience in his voice, "Boy! this one debt for which your father is security is but one of many. If I would sell this home and all its belongings it would not pay the thousandth part."

Poor John began to realize the hopelessness of his appeal. "But surely there is something you can do; something left of all your great property."

"Nothing; all is in the hands of the creditors." Then he half started as if a sudden remembrance had come to him.

"Then, Mr. Newton," and John drew himself up, "I call you to remember there is a God, and He is the God of my father and mother," and with that he left the presence of the man who had caused so much trouble in his home.

The youth paused for a moment in his homeward ride. Before him stretched the loved acres of his childhood's home—his no longer. Back of him on the banks of the Illinois towered the great mill which had been such a source of wealth to its owner.

"Well, old farm! go from us for a time if you will, but some day I'll win you back. Yes, and more," and he looked squarely at the mill which was just now being lighted by the evening sun. Then touching Beauty he cantered home.

William Newton watched the boyish figure as it recklessly strode down the graveled walk.

"Yes, it is hard for them," he said softly. "Could I buy peace of conscience if I gave them the deed to the one thing left me? So poor, that the hungry creditors did not care to bother with it. Those acres of arid waste in Arizona; I thought they would have yielded me gold. 'Twas but another bubble. At any rate they shall see that I have done all that I could."

So saying he went to a drawer, drew out an envelope and with a few strokes of the pen, made John Stevenson the owner of a tract of desert land in Arizona.

Putting it into an envelope he wrote a note to John Stevenson, telling him he hoped that in the years to come he would think differently of him.

Just then a servant called him to his wife's **bedside.**

She was dying.

About the hour that the Stevensons received **William Newton's** communication, they also received **the news** that Margaret, his wife, had **passed beyond the** pale of human praise or censure.

"**No, it** is worthless, absolutely worthless; you may as well toss it into the open grate." John Stevenson like a drowning man catching at a straw, had gone to a lawyer, asking him to accept for the debt the deed of the western land and received for reply the above answer.

With a heavy heart he turned to leave. Suddenly **a sense of the hopelessness of** his cause **swept over him, and a despair he** had not known **seized him, and in a** moment the worthless paper which **had brought him** this fresh disappointment, lay upon the smouldering coals of the grate.

So burdened was he that he did not observe that **his youngest** son, who had accompanied him, as quickly stooped and removing it from **its** perilous position placed it in his own pocket. But the lawyer did, and smiled at the **boy's** independence of action as well as **at the** shrewdness displayed.

Rachel awaited his return and read the result of his visit in his face.

It was, "we must find another home!" In after years they wondered how they ever lived through the trying days.

Added to the thought of leaving their home, was the pertinent query, where should they turn? What should they do? It had been hard to make a living on the farm, to rent one seemed a doubtful experiment.

It was found that while they would lose the farm they would be able to keep the stock.

These it was decided to sell, and if possible get a home in Burton. And then, how should they live? This question both Rachel and John turned over again and again in their minds.

Jerome Mills was a member of the same church as the Stevensons, and was the grocer in Burton with whom the family had always dealt.

He was possessed of a great longing to live in the country, which desire became intensified by the sight of golden rolls of butter, the baskets of fresh eggs and other farm produce which Rachel was wont to bring in each week in exchange for groceries.

Hearing from Lawyer Nevins that the Stevenson farm was to be rented, he at once went to see if they could not make a trade.

They soon arrived at a conclusion. The stock, excepting that belonging to the children, should remain on the farm, the property of Mr. Mills, while the Stevensons should take his grocery business and rent his house; an untried venture, still it might prove successful.

John Stevenson was not a man to delay matters, so when he abandoned all hope, he at once made preparations for the inevitable, and a few days later two large wagons stood in the grassy lane, into which the household effects were packed.

Poor Rachel! But a month ago, with a light heart she had planned to move into the new rooms, but now strangers would enjoy the comfort she had never known! Yet it was not for these she most sorrowed. Here in the great kitchen, at the table, the merry group of boys and girls had gathered and spent the meal time in laughter and repartee. Here about this hearth her little children had played. In that little bedroom Asbury had been converted, but why call up the past.

Like as unto the Israelites of old, the command had come to go forward, she could trust that now, as then, there would be a pillar of fire to lead, so without a tear, (for her husband's sake) brave Rachel Stevenson went out from the home of her early wifehood and motherhood.

All were ready to go, but the boy John could nowhere be found.

Guided by a mother's instinct, Rachel went herself to the barn, and there in the manger of Beauty's stall, with his arms about the wondering animal's

neck, poor John was giving away to the wild abandonment of grief.

The sight moved his mother as nothing else, and
sitting down they wept together. But time moves
inexorably on and pays little heed to tears and the
pawing teams were ready to start, so at last they
rose to go, when John, who looked like a hero—
even in his blue shirt and cotton pants—said, "I'll
have it back, every acre of it; every acre of it."

A few days after they had gotten settled they
were surprised by a call from the director of what
had been their home school. He soon made his
errand known. It was that their township had
requested the services of Ruth to teach the spring
school. This young lady at first demurred on
account of fancied inability, but yielded, and erelong seemed to have found her niche in the plain
little school room.

Edward remained in the Academy, while John
found enough to keep him busy helping his father
get adjusted to the new work of the store.

Like a patient mother bird that sees its nest
broken and despoiled, yet patiently goes to work to
repair the breach, so this other mother began the
work of building a new home, under surroundings
so different from the past.

The task was not so hard after all, for had they
not each other? and it was with genuine sorrow that
they thought of the lonely man in the great house,
who weeks before had sadly followed his beautiful

12

Margaret out from the door of her **luxurious home**
to the stillness of the grave.

Richard had come to his mother's burial, and **after**
coming home from the last sad rites he learned **for
the** first time **of the** Stevenson's loss. He was
shocked, overwhelmed, and felt this more than the
loss of his father's entire fortune.

How could Louise forgive this? Would not the
very name of Newton be the synonym for everything despicable? How he longed in the few days
of his stay to go to the farmhouse and express his
sympathy and sorrow, but he durst not. He
resolved, though, as it seemed best for him to finish
his collegiate year, that on his return he would stop
at the University and learn his fate from the lips of
her who, now that such sorrows had swept in **on**
him, seemed all that was left of life.

His heart, yes, **and his pride mourned for
Therese, for** she had **been** his favorite. He could
have **borne** without a murmur the mere loss of
property for youth is strong, brave and hopeful, but
then came the death of his mother, that beautiful,
gracious being whose life had been the one question, "What will make my children most happy?"

She may have erred in answering the question,
but kindness, love and gentleness had marked her
rule, and over her coffin Richard first **tasted** the
bitterness of sorrow.

It would be hard **to depict the sorrow, the indig-**

nation and the anxiety which both Asbury and Louise carried in their hearts in these days.

To give up the home, the fruit of honest toil, for another, to go out into the world well nigh penniless! Imagination refused to take in the thought that now, at this very time, the family were leaving the old home. Each felt that to remain in school was out of the question. If they were home, surely they might help in some way. This they wrote.

Promptly came the message from father and mother, "The one bit of silver lining to this cloud is that you are each so nearly ready for your life work. If you love us, stay where you are, and make the most of each day. This thought will bear us up as nothing else will."

The wisdom of this was apparent, but they could scarcely study harder than before, for they were already known among the best of the University.

As Louise was going to her room from recitation, one day about a week after the receipt of the news from home, a note was handed to her. It read:

"LOUISE: I have been to my mother's burial. I cannot go back to school without seeing you. You have a right to hate our very name, but will you not see me? RICHARD."

Louise read, wondering. Could it be? "His mother dead, and he in town? And he thinks I blame him. Poor, unhappy Richard! No! What

had he to do with this? Nothing." And with a
longing to look into his face, she wrote:

"Dear Richard: Come."

An hour later these two, the current of whose
lives had flown together since childhood and which
in these later years had been indissolubly knit together in that strange tie, stronger than death itself,
which for lack of a better word we call "love,"
were together.

Richard had been moved deeper than he knew
by the sad succession of events of the past few
weeks, and it was no unmanly thing that on catching sight of the bright true face so dear to him,
and just now radiant with the divine light of sympathy, he should sink into a chair and weep again,
as he had, over his mother's coffin.

Then began the divine ministry of woman's love
to bind up the bruised and broken hearted.

Tenderly she drew from him the story of his
mother's death, of which she had not heard. With
tact she made him understand that she imputed no
intentional wrong to the sorrowing father, who now
was certainly an object of pity to the most careless.

With a hope she hardly dared feel she pictured
the future of her own father and mother, and
urged him to make the most of himself by making
the most of the remaining months in college.

How she longed to ask him if in these sorrows
he had gone to the great Source of comfort, but she
remembered that if such matters were not actually

scoffed at, they were held with indifference by members of the Newton home.

Well, in later years he should learn her own sweet faith.

Foolish Louise! A thousand unhappy wives would bear testimony to the futility of that hope.

Listening to her, Richard felt his dejection slipping away. Yes, life was still rich, for it held Louise.

He told her how in another year he would enter a law office. "And, Louise," said he, "believe me, my first care shall be to see that this loss of yours shall be made good."

As he read in her eyes the devotion of her heart, a great sense of shame swept over him that he was not more worthy of her. Looking into her eyes, how easy seemed the right. Ah, how he hated Braceton; how like a Nemesis arose the remembrance of the hours spent in his company.

He was not going until a late evening train. There was to be an open meeting of the Literary Society to which Louise belonged, and to change the sad drift of his thoughts she insisted that he attend. She had promised a song for the occasion, and for more than a week had been practicing the high warbling notes of a solo in a new popular opera. Scarcely had the last note died away when the vigorous prolonged encore gave her the coveted opportunity, and the rich clear voice took up that blessed hymn of comfort which has soothed

so many sorrowing ones, "Come ye disconsolate."
As she sang,

> "Earth has no sorrow
> That heaven cannot heal,"

little wonder that the company listened in awe at the
pathos, for with every note there was a prayer that
her lover might test this truth for himself. Sitting
there, unconscious of the prayer, Richard resolved
to do this very thing, and from this very hour to
live an earnest Christian life. Alas, had it not
been for Braceton; alas, had it not been for the
inexorable reaping from the sowings of the past.

CHAPTER XVII.

GETTING SETTLED—LIFE IN A COLLEGE CLUB.

SPRINGTIME had come, and other hands than the Stevensons were sowing the home acres. It is always hard for a man late in life to change his business; it was doubly so for John Stevenson.

Brought up on a farm, spending his life there, in that place he was at home, but as for a "store," he felt out of place, awkward, having scarcely any adaptability for it, but something had to be done, and this had seemed to be the "something" that offered.

If this were true of himself, it was hardly so with the boys. Edward had remained in the Academy, it being his last year, but there were the long mornings and evenings, which he took largely to familiarize himself with the new business, and gradually the whole of the book-keeping fell into his hands.

John became in this new business his father's most valued helper. At first he chafed at the confinement and groaned in his soul as he longed to be on the farm again. But he soon began to develop genuine business instinct, and, young as he was, his father learned to rely upon him as the purchaser of supplies. Known to all his acquaintances as a man of sterling honesty, having their sympathy in his loss, it was not strange that customers flocked to the new venture and that erelong the mere question of an honest living was assured.

Nor did the wife find the task of adjusting herself to the new home a difficult one. It will be remembered the coveted new rooms at the farmhouse had been unoccupied. The Mills' home was a new and well built cottage, with much more room and many more conveniences than she had known. "But, alas!" thought both she and her husband, "to live in a home that is not our own."

Yet the home touches were not long in asserting themselves, nor the living room in taking on a cozy home air. There were two good-sized southern windows which before many months what with hanging vines and blooming flowers were marvels of beauty. Between these were arranged the shelves for books. And from these, their old worn friends—the books of the year's gathering—soon greeted them, and their greeting seemed well nigh human. Ah, they had not lost all. Indeed, though everything else should have been swept away, the past with its rich associations was forever theirs. And with that past, indeed one of its strongest factors, were these same silent friends who had now followed them into the uncertainties of the present.

In a corner of the room Edward's individual tastes asserted themselves. In a cabinet of his own making, with a plain glass front, was his collection of botanical specimens. One more deeply skilled than he might have called many of these worthless, but in their broadening, educating influence upon the boy himself in the sweet spell which their collecting had thrown over him, keeping him from possible rude associates and in opening to him the riches of nature, Rachel would have been slow to pronounce the most insignificant one worthless.

Accustomed on the farm to much "outside work," the home keeping in the Mills' home seemed a very light affair, and it was well, for the years together with the events of the last few months were telling plainly on the strong factor of the whole, the house mother.

As for the college students, it had been hard for them to remain at their post amid all these harrowing changes, but the home commands were imperative. Yet each felt something must be done. But what? Asbury's expenses were already at a minimum, thanks to the student club of which he was a member, but Louise with Emma had found a delightfully congenial home which had opened its doors to the students and where she had remained during her entire stay in the college. But why should she not try Asbury's plan? That which she

most dreaded was the losing of Emma's sweet
companionship, for without the slightest need for
economy there would be little use for her to take
any discomfort upon herself.

Among the worshippers at the same church with
Louise was a very tall, angular woman with that
peculiar snappy kind of black eyes which seem to
be continually upon the lookout for a fault. Her
husband had grown tired of life years before, and
left her with the care of a large family, all girls,
and a bit of property in the country. She had
sold her country property and invested in an old
rambling house in the town whose only recommen-
dation was the great number of rooms it contained. She had hoped to earn her livelihood in
the time-honored way of keeping boarders, but
there were so many cheery homes open was it
any wonder the students passed this sharp-visaged
woman and her roomy house by? Her latest
ambition had been to organize a "girl's club,"
whereby college expenses might be considerably
lessened for girls as well as their brothers. Indeed,
at the time when Louise began to cast about for a
plan to economize, a small club of the kind was
already in operation.

Perhaps it may be as well to state here that
owing to the wise foresight of her father in his
plan for the "college fund," this was fortunately
not necessary, yet with the air of a martyr Louise
went on a tour of inspection, feeling very grand

and self-sacrificing. The outlook at Mrs. Hoyson's (the club manager) seemed dreary enough, even for the most pronounced martyrdom, but this suited her present mood better than sunshine and cheer, and as she might have signed her own death warrant she made the arrangements for the change.

There remained yet one task itself, of no small magnitude, and that was to acquaint Emma with her decision.

That evening the girls were sitting in their cosy room, apparently busy in the lessons for the next day. After Louise had gotten up the seventh time to punch a fire that was already glowing brightly, and had walked several times to the window and beaten a tattoo on the panes, Emma tossed her book aside and said, "You might as well out with it whatever it is. Have you in a sudden gust of passion murdered some one, and is the wraith making you uncomfortable? Come, unburden your heart to the one that loves you." Emma had struck a mock heroic attitude, and seemed to be listening intently for a confession she expected would chill the very marrow in her bones.

Louise smiled, a kind of wan smile it must be admitted, how she began and how she ended she never knew, but in some way or other an idea of the proposed change began at length to dawn upon Emma, and really if the "marrow" was not frozen

as she had expected, she was quite as much excited
as if such an event had really occurred.

"Can it be possible," thought she, "that the old·
sweet companionship is to be broken up?" No,
never; and greatly to the surprise of Louise, after
her excited roommate had taken two or three turns
about the room she stopped squarely in front of her
and announced her intention of accompanying her.
A swift vision of the plain, meagerly furnished room
she had just secured passed rapidly before her, and
mentally she contrasted it with the luxurious one in
Emma's own home. Then there was the vinegar-
ish Mrs. Hoyson, the new landlady. Louise
wearily acknowledged to herself that in all probability herein would lie the greatest trial of the new
life. No, Emma must not make this sacrifice; thus
much she said, but Emma remained firm.

"Now you need not say a word, my mind is fully
made up. Let me tell you something. Do you
remember last summer at one of the meetings of
the Missionary Band, Mrs. Millionaire was urging
us to exercise self-denial in our gifts, showing so
plainly that the Lord took a special delight in such
giving. I remember to have felt a sense of shame
that in all my life I had not known what it was to
really do without something I wanted in order to
get money to give. Now here is my opportunity.
I will go with you to the club, and every dollar so
saved (and I will keep an exact account) shall go

to that new mission in the interior of China. Now it is settled."

And so it was. A few days later found the friends unpacking their "penates," as in schoolgirl fashion they styled their trunks, and few other belongings, in one of the grim, bare rooms belonging to Mrs. Hoyson.

A square of rag carpet ornamented the floor of this room, while a bed, a washstand, a plain table and two chairs comprised the furniture. The windows were small and nearer the ceiling than the floor. The views from neither were enspiriting. In front some busy men—in a cooper shop—kept up a a rat-tat-tat on some barrels the whole day long, while from the rear the view was excellent of a cemetery about a block away. Far from this being an occasion of worrying, however, it became the subject of many an odd remark from Emma, and notwithstanding the dreariness of the place not a day passed without the sound of happy girlish laughter. Looking back upon their college lives in after years, two sober women, each seriously intent upon performing the duties with which their lives became singularly full, were wont to smile as episode after episode of this happy—supremely *funny* club life was recalled.

If Mrs. Hoyson, had one feature predominant above another that feature was neatness, her white aprons were always smooth and glossy in their stiffness, and woe to the unlucky roomer who

left things " lying around." Emma and Louise took
turns in " straightening."   One morning, it being
Emma's turn (Louise was at her practice), that
young lady concluded she would hurry up her fire
and took some oil from the lamp to do so.   Great
was her dismay to find a great oil spot on the floor.
What would Mrs. Hoyson say? Now Emma really
knew nothing of housework and as she stood con-
templating the spot, " Why not burn it off," something seemed to suggest.   Well, in the next minute
she learned a thing or two about how *not* to
remove a grease spot.   The " fire " was promptly
put out, but not until the girls had gathered from
the different rooms with Mrs. Hoyson, grim and
severe, at their lead.   Poor Emma, she hardly
knew which was most to be dreaded, the " oh mys"
of the girls or the stony displeasure of Mrs. Hoyson.

The plan of the present campaign of economics
was that there should be one of their number who
in their turn should do the purchasing of supplies,
and it became a matter of rivalry to see which
could bring their expenses down to the lowest possible figure and yet maintain a good bill of fare.
However, it became tacitly understood, if either
of these points were to be sacrificed, the uncomplaining latter should be the victim.   That year,
as if to get ready for such emergencies nature had
sent a bountiful crop of potatoes, and never before
had either Louise or Emma dreamed of the possibilities of this one mealy jacketed tuber.

It became quite an experience with Emma to go with pencil and note book in hand, and with an air of importance make the acquaintance of grocers and butchers, and exchange animated remarks upon the lowest possible price of vegetables or meat, and none learned quicker than she the possibilities of a soup bone or the satisfying qualities of a breakfast of batter cakes.

This last knowledge came from a remark of Mrs. Hoyson herself, with whom Emma was arranging the breakfasts for her week, and discussing the merits of the various breakfast dishes proposed, always of course with an eye to economy. Mrs. Hoyson, to help matters along, ventured the remark with her peculiar nasal drawl and without much regard to grammar or pronunciation, "You'd better try pancakes; pancakes is mighty fillin'." This Emma, with her inimitable sense of humor, related for the benefit of the club, and pancakes became the order of the day.

Having tasted the sweets of economy, Emma began to carry it into her private expenses, as the following will show: They were all seated at the table when Louise happened to remark, "I wish we had a barrel of apples, say of Belleflower, or of Winesaps from the home orchard."

"Oh, dear," returned Emma, "Apples are dreadful dear. I priced some on the way to school this morning, and they were three for a dime." I wanted some so badly though I told the boy I would take *five cents worth*." A peal of laughter followed this announcement, and it took Emma a whole minute to discover that there was anything funny in the proposed purchase of half an apple. "No wonder the boy looked perplexed and busied himself with another customer," she admitted to herself.

A full account of all these exploits Emma "wrote up" in her weekly letter home. At first these letters were a source of great amusement, and much interest was felt in "Emma's latest freak." After awhile, however, the fear came that perhaps for the sake of health the girls were carrying the matter too far, and so upon the receipt of the apple episode done up in Emma's most melo-dramatic manner, Mrs. Ward said emphatically, "Well, I have wanted to visit Emma for a long time. I am going at once."

A few days after, as the girls were sitting down to one of their plainest dinners, they were greatly surprised by seeing a cab drive up, and in another moment Emma was in her mother's arms. It did not take that lady long to decide that both Emma and Louise would be better off back in their old cosy home. Mr. Ward sent a message to the effect that he would see that Mrs. Millionaire and the mission did not suffer in this decision. Louise concurred, with a bit of exultation in her heart, it must be confessed. Besides, had she not had an "experience" as well as the home folks?

CHAPTER XVIII.

AN ORATORICAL CONTEST—SAD ENDING.

IN pleasanter quarters the year passed, and never perhaps had more genuine hard work been done. Commencement week was hastening, but preceding this by a fortnight an event was to occur in which the interest of all centered.

Their university was a member of an intercollegiate oratorical association, and had been chosen as the place where representatives of the different colleges should meet and contest for the honor of supremacy.

With a thrill of pride Louise received from Richard the message that he had been chosen to represent his college. Ah if he should win! and her blood hasted and her cheeks glowed as she imagined him the hero of the occasion. Little else than the contest was talked of. At length the day came.

As the representatives from the different colleges began to gather, it was easy to see that they were all picked men, the pride of their institutions. Many

13

were accompanied by some of their particular friends who desired to witness the success, as each one hoped, of their "man."

Among them came Richard Newton, who lost no time in calling upon her for whose sake he was most anxious to succeed. From him Louise learned that a company of his friends, among whom was a Mr. Braceton, had accompanied him.

The next few hours seemed like a dream, they were so full of feverish anxiety. At length came the packed hall, the flutter of college colors, the din of college yells, and then the genuine eloquence of each contestant.

Presently a clear, rich, well modulated voice began. Ah! how well Louise knew each tone. See, the audience is growing still, is bending to listen.

The chosen theme is one that touches the heart, and the great heart of the audience responds as the earnest, impassioned sentences fall from the speaker's lips.

The orator at length sits down amid a storm of applause. There were others yet to speak, but Louise felt that her lover had won, and it was true.

Later the prize was given to him, a lovely silvered head of the great Demosthenes, crowned with a golden crown of laurel, the latter of such fine and beautiful workmanship that the delicate leaves seemed to quiver before the slightest breeze.

Louise could not trust herself to offer the customary congratulations, before many curious eyes.

Leaving a message with Asbury to the effect that she and her roommate, Miss Ward, would call in the morning, she quickly sought the privacy of her room.

In the after years of her life she was wont to look back upon the delirious joy of that evening as of an experience in the life of another, one of whom perhaps she had read, so far away and unreal did it come to seem.

Her first thought on awakening the next morning was, "Richard has won!" How proud she felt of him. What might she not expect from the future in which the world must recognize his ability?

In front of her window stood a great tree, always a favorite trysting place for robins and the other birds of the locality. As she threw open the sash she noticed a robin swaying to and fro on one of the topmost boughs. As she looked she saw him throw back his head, and in an ecstacy of delight burst into such a flood of melody that the quiet stillness of the morning seemed suddenly to become one great anthem of praise. This accorded well with her own present emotions, and she said softly to herself, " The bird is not happier than I."

The song finished, the happy songster flew up yet a little higher and perched upon another limb, not yet leaving the shady tree. Suddenly there was a whirr from a bow and arrow in the hands of a neighbor's boy, and his sweet song was hushed forever.

Shocked, and with her heart filled with pity at the tragedy, she hastened to where he lay gasping, but as she stroked the ruffled plumage, there was no voice to whisper that her own happiness might be wrecked as quickly.

As she knew that in all probability many would call at the victor's rooms during the morning, she arranged that hers should be as early as possible, and so as the silvery chimes of ten o'clock rang out, she with Asbury and Emma started for the hotel where he was stopping.

Let us for a moment go back to the victor. Flushed with excitement, congratulated on all sides, the idol for the time of the college friends who had accompanied him, Richard Newton went to his rooms happier, having lately known such sorrow, than he could have dreamed possible.

Students from the different colleges began to gather in his room and offer congratulations. Later when the number had narrowed down to perhaps a half dozen, Braceton suggested that they should celebrate the victory in some sort of style.

Richard demurred. More than once in Braceton's own room he had gone beyond the bounds, and none knew as well as he the danger that menaced him. But Braceton insisted and finally a bottle of champagne was brought.

" No, no, not here," Richard said as the spark-
ling glass was handed him.

At this arose a laugh which was decisive—it
is easier for some souls to stand before a bullet
than before a laugh—so the glass was drained,
then 'another. Other bottles were brought, and
soon the walls echoed with foolish laughter and
jest.

With the second draught all control of himself
passed from young Newton. Gone were the
memories of a mother's death, a father's trouble,
gone even the memory of Louise; and not until
the early dawn did he fall into a drunken stupor,
dressed as he had come from the hall, and so he
was lying when Louise crossed the threshold.

The parlors of this hotel were on the second
floor, and the room Richard and Braceton occupied
was only a door distant.

On the arrival of the visitors the porter knocked
at the door, handed the card to Braceton who
had answered. (It was a peculiarity that the drink
that would affect the quick, nervous brain of
Newton, Braceton would hardly feel.)

As he took the card he read aloud the name.
Was it the magic of the name that broke the
drunken stupor? At any rate, Richard slowly
arose, looked wildly around saying, " Where am
I ?"

" Pull yourself together, old fellow," said Braceton. "You have callers that I think you would

like to see, though you had better say you're out till you're in better shape."

"What do you say?" and as he seized the delicate card in his hand, somehow, through the befogged brain was borne the fact that Louise was waiting, and without a moment's hesitation he started to go to her.

Perceiving this, Braceton took hold of him to hold him back. Then came the sound of a thick, incoherent, angry voice, echoes of which floated over the open transom into the parlors. Emma started, and Louise grew pale with apprehension.

Suddenly the door opened, and in walked Richard, with hair wildly dishevelled, eyes bloodshot, his whole attire bespeaking a night's carousal.

Muttering something in an incoherent, unsteady manner, he essayed to walk across the room to where Louise sat, the strong odor of wine preceding him.

Like a flash upon the startled girl came the memory of that dreadful night when Baby Flossie lay dying, and a drunken husband had ended his own miserable life; and with this flash came a realizing sense of Richard's condition.

With a low moan and a startled, appealing glance toward Asbury and Emma, she fled through the open door.

Oh! to be home, to be in her own room, to be anywhere that she might hide her shame and disgrace.

A few minutes later, returning homeward, she
entered the gateway, and just by the door the body
of the dead robin still lay. Mechanically she stopped as she said, "Oh! little bird, I am brought as
low as you; your happiness is not more surely
ended than is mine."

Passing to her room, the disgrace of the scene
she had so recently witnessed well nigh overwhelmed her. With it came the conviction, slow
but sure, that the various whispered rumors which
had reached her during the years, and to which she
had so vehemently refused credence were true.
Then came the pain and the heart agony as the
idol came to be torn out, for "torn from her heart
he should be," she said to herself. An hour ago
she had been so proud of him; but now? yes, the
dream was over. Little Flossie had not died in
vain.

The next day the great panting engine rapidly
bore Louise on her homeward journey, yet it could
not go fast enough to suit the wild tumult in her
heart. After what seemed an age the familiar
home depot was reached. She had half expected
that her father or one of the boys would meet her,
else how would she get out to the farm?

. A sudden remembrance of the change swept
over her. Ordering a carriage she was soon being
driven rapidly to the new home.

Rachel had been unusually busy that morning,
and had just sat down in an easy chair for a few

minutes talk with her husband who had entered
when hearing the noise of wheels at the gate, and
glancing out she caught sight of the carriage which
she recognized as one that carried passengers to
and from the trains.

"Why! who can it be?" and she looked curiously
at the strangely familiar figure now coming up the
walk.

As Louise stepped upon the porch she raised
her veil as if in search of something familiar. As
Rachel looked on the face, and recognized it as her
daughter's, a sudden fear swept over her.

"Louise, Louise! my child, speak, tell me, are
you ill?" for Louise was now sobbing—the first
tears since that dreadful morning.

"Yes, mother, sick of life, sick at heart."

Gently Rachel unloosed her wraps and removed
her hat, and with motherly tact soothed her while
she told the dreadful story.

"Mother," said Louise, after the storm had spent
itself and she had been soothed by the sympathy
of both father and mother, "it is all over. Henceforth he is to me as if he had never been. I can
never forget poor little Flossie."

At this, though her face betokened naught but
true sympathy with the grief of her daughter, a
song of thanksgiving arose in the mother's heart.
Curiously enough, even as she held her in her arms
and comforted her, the night of her own agony in
the farm house came vividly back. How, torn

with doubts and fears, she had tossed upon her bed, saying over and over to herself, "It must be broken off ; but how?" Alas that in the answering there should be so many ruined hopes and so much of sorrow.

To do her justice, it must be said that she was grieved to hear Richard's fall. She had not expected it to come in so gross a manner. She had yielded at last a tacit consent to the marriage which seemed inevitable, but with all her intuitions on the alert she could see nothing but unhappiness. Better a thousand heartaches at present, she said to herself as she noted Louise's grief, than that the entire life should be wrecked, and trusting to the elasticity of youth, she hoped that all would yet be well.

After the first greetings, and the first pangs of shame and grief over, Louise quickly detected the changes time had brought about. Her father looked old and careworn, and there came a realizing sense in her heart of all the dear ones had suffered, and the hope was born and grew that though her own happiness was as she believed wrecked forever, still there might remain the joy of lightening their burdens.

The greatest change was in her brothers and sisters. She could hardly connect the old quiet playmate Ruth with the tall, slender, girlish woman who ruled with a sway of gentleness in the little schoolhouse just back of the farm.

Edward and John seemed suddenly grown up, the latter a counterpart of his father. Indeed, sometimes as he walked down the yard there was that in his carriage that brought back strangely to Rachel the old days at Lynton when a shy, rugged farmer had become all in all to her. He had his father's strict notions of honesty and his mother's unquestioning faith, and with the advantage of a modern education he bade fair to make him a widely useful man. But it was a matter of regret that he seemed less inclined to study than the others. There had been so much hard work on the farm, always something for which he seemed especially fitted; so it was not strange that he was not the student that either of the older ones were.

A letter soon followed Louise from Asbury, in which he stated that he had received an offer to take charge of a congregation in the State where the University was situated. So with his parents' leave he would not be home during the vacation, and Louise was the more readily reconciled to this because, while he sympathized with her in the mortification which she had endured, yet with his strict notions of right and wrong, he had always agreed with his mother that there could be nothing but unhappiness from the marriage, and really he felt that no price was too dear to pay for release from such a bondage.

The father and mother began though to wonder if their children would ever be at home together again.

CHAPTER XIX.

" FAREWELL, LIFE CHOICE."

OUISE soon found her niche in the household. She had lost none of her old helpfulness, and as Ruth's school was just closing, the mother would say jesting that with two grown daughters her occupation was gone.

She found the family still sore over the loss of their home, yet bravely trying to make the best of life. As for herself—she did not dare let them know how much she missed the dear old home and the farm, with the many associations of her childhood, nor how much of a stranger she felt herself to be in the smart new cottage they were beginning to call home.

In those days she did not look far into the future. The past had been so bitter, perhaps it might be given her in the every day life of the present to be of some practical use to her brothers and sisters. So with as much zeal as though her livelihood depended upon it she began giving Ruth instruction in music. Edward's rapid development had startled her, and it was with genuine pride that she noted his well defined literary taste. She often said to her parents as she noted his unerring judgment of the literature which came into the home, that certainly somewhere and somehow he would find his life-work among books, but how should she interest John, rugged, plain-spoken, practical John, upon whom the family were coming to lean more and more, for that he must be interested in books and in study she felt very sure.

Now fortune favored her; quite a bit of local interest was manifest just now in the application of certain phosphates to a stretch of alkaline lands which ran up to one side of the city, and none were more interested than John in the outcome. This gave her an idea. Might he not become interested in chemistry itself? She approached the question with tact, and ere long it came to be the usual thing to have an " experiment " on hands. One victory won she planned another. She had many interesting episodes of her class studies in geology with which she regaled him as they took tramp after tramp, of her planning together. Yes, they really littered up the house, and brought home much that was worthless, but a nature hitherto deaf to the persuasive voice of study was surely awakening, and Louise, fresh from a realm where learning and culture were sovereign, felt no trouble too great if that goal could be reached.

It was not strange that occasionally on these tramps their feet should turn toward the old farm.

One day as they sat together on the edge of the woodland Louise remembered so well, John recounted for his sister's benefit the whole history of those dreadful weeks. So vivid was his portrayal that she seemed to live over the scene, and could almost hear the creak of the wagons that bore the family and belongings away.

"But I tell you sister mine, I'll have every acre back," and as he spoke his glowing face and flashing eye showed that this promise which he had made to himself and his mother in the midst of their trouble had taken deep root in his heart. Louise watched the strong face, and began to question him as to his plans. These she found were as yet very vague, but here was her opportunity, and in a kindly way she showed that in order to cope with the world an education was necessary. "But I'll never go to college," insisted he.

"Well, you need not if you so choose, but a certain amount of education you must have. Take mathematics for instance——" "Don't mention that study; it is the prince of all evils," interposed John.

"By no means, rather this science is mankind's best friend," and she went on to tell him among other things, of the wonderful array of facts that would be absolutely unknowable without this science. His interest was aroused, and before another week had passed he had gotten the key to successful study—*he was interested*—and in after

years when an ocean came to roll between these
two, this sweet companionship became a blessed
memory. Nor did this gifted sister with all the
later work that she was permitted to do in after
years, ever value aught of that so highly as she did
these few weeks spent with her brother.

A few weeks after Louise's return an event
occurred which, in order to properly chronicle, we
shall have to return to the university so suddenly
and unceremoniously left.

Never did Esau of old sorrow more over the loss
of his birthright than did Richard Newton when he
came to himself and realized what had occurred.

Shame, mortification, s e l f condemnation and
anger at the false friends raged in his breast. With
intellectual, laurel-crowned brow his " Demosthenes " gazed solemnly at him from the mantle.
How he hated the unoffending silver. What were
a thousand prizes if disgrace ruled supreme and
Louise were lost.

Braceton flippantly bade him " cheer up." To
Richard's credit be it said, he angrily turned on
him and bade him begone; he wished never to see
him again.

Was all lost ? Gradually the hope grew upon
him that it was not. He knew that Louise's great
love had stood firm in the other great trials.
Might he not hope it would yet stand ? He
turned this over, and at last resolved to go
and throw himself upon her mercy. He knew of

her sudden flight home, he could guess her mortification, but there was but one hope in life left him.
He would see her, would plead his case, and give
her his solemn pledge that he would never again
touch wine in any form.

How clearly he now saw, with her, that this was
for him the only safe course.

One day in the early summer, Louise was
startled by the appearance of her lover. She dared
not look at him lest the sight of his abject sorrow
might turn her.

"Never again would he fall so low," came the
promise straight from the heart, for the pleader
knew that for him it was a matter of life or death.

With her by his side, he was sure he could
stand; without her he was lost. But no; she could
not listen. She had to bid him go, for a dead baby
face looked out from a bank of flowers bidding her
remember that " a drunkard is a slave."

So these two parted, the one to go to her room
to throw herself upon the hard floor in agony, to
moan, to pray, and finally from her knees to go out
bravely into life to take up such duties as He might
give. The other? as Adam left Paradise, to that
may this other going be likened. Behind were
love and happiness, and he told himself, success.
Beyond? but he could get no further, for despair
lay at his heart. *He knew he was lost.*

Did she do right? Was not her place at his side,
if in happiness? Well, if in suffering still the

same? Ought she not to have thrown her pure, strong self in the breach, in an effort to save this erring, brilliant young man?

Ask the drunkard's child who begs at your doorway, half clad, hungry, often diseased in body, an imbecile in mind; ask the drunkard's wife as hungry, beaten, bruised, she pitifully stoops on the common to gather a few sticks to warm her babes, while she goes to beg charity that they may be fed. Ask, if you still doubt, the murdered Flossies (and they are many), and in one strong chorus the answer comes, "*She did right!*"

' After Richard's departure, until near the close of the Summer, the days went by without incident. Louise, with the old imperiousness all gone, anxious for a work that might help her to forget her sorrow, entered heartily into the duties of the home. She often contrasted this Summer with the last; that so full of the world, and this of home quiet. One day, toward the end of August, a letter came to her from Emma's home, but the superscription was not Emma's.

She broke the seal and read with growing interest and surprise, then handed it in silence to her father.

It proved to be from Mrs. Millionaire, who wrote not only in loving remembrance, but in referring to the pleasant acquaintance of a year ago said: "You will remember my brother William, who was in theological school when you were here. He and

his wife have been accepted as missionaries to a
province in China. The Woman's Union Missionary society is earnestly calling for a consecrated
young woman to go with them to teach in a school.
Indeed, I shall have to say plainly, to build up from
nothing a girl's college. I have had you in my
mind as a suitable person. Will you go? Shall I
present your name as a candidate?"

The letter dropped from John Stevenson's hands
as he finished reading it aloud to his wife. How
often about their hearthstone had foreign missionaries been earnestly prayed for. Many were the
sacrifices that had been made that they might have
more for this beloved cause. But to give a daughter, and she one who had throughout her life been
in a peculiar sense the brightness, the sunshine, the
music of the home! How could it be? And
Louise? See her as she stands there by the window ledge, her face a study of emotions. So resolutely had she thrust away her cup of proffered happiness, and so uncomplainingly had she busied herself about the home, that not one of the household
had realized the real depth of the blow under which
she staggered.

It is a strange fact that parents are often slow to
ascribe the same depth of feeling to their children
which they themselves p o s s e s s. To illustrate:
Rachel Stevenson's children never tired of hearing
her tell of the dear old village of Lynton, of the
old sweet days when she and their father became

14

all in all to each other, of their wedding day and of
the strange journey westward. As the boys and
girls grew older, often one would say to the other,
"How much mother must have loved father to
have left her friends and home forever," and though
Rachel had not seemed to suspect it, just such a
love had Louise felt for Richard Newton. Thoughts
of him had entered into every phase of her life.
When she had practiced a song, running all
through and giving zest to the practice had been
thoughts of her bonny young lover. Ah, how
brilliant he was, how hard she must work for his
sake! This self abnegation of true love must
alawys remain one of the wonders of the human
heart. Yet loving him so, she had relentlessly at
duty's bidding, uttered the words that had parted
them forever. She was too brave and sensible,
though, to allow her life to become a failure, so she
had thrown herself with all her energies into the
duties that had happened to lie nearest. But oh,
the heart hunger, the ache, and the pity. The one
cry of her heart had been for work, absorbing
work, and now came this call. Was it of God?
Was she worthy? Her heart bounded at the
thought. If these two questions were but settled
how gladly she would go. She had told her
parents much concerning her work and study during the past summer as member of the mission
circle. Could it be they thought, as they noted
her eagerness to go, that that had been a providen-

tial school sent before by the Father to prepare this child of His for service. If so—no; but it could not be settled without Help, but the Help so freely promised for every need was given, and after a week, in what seemed in its heart agony to be an echo of Gethsemane this Christian father and mother were able, through their tears, to say "go."

Perhaps never did weeks slip by as did these few intervening between the date fixed for her departure. Asbury hastened home, that they might all be together again. So with aching hearts father and mother saw the dawn of the day that was to take their darling away, yet not one would have uttered the word "*stay.*"

Louise never forgot the last morning, as they gathered for family prayers. How old, how bent, seemed her father, as with trembling voice he began to read those matchless words of David, "He that dwelleth in the secret places of the Most High shall abide under the shelter of his wings." From the beginning John and Rachel Stevenson had been so careful about nothing as that they and theirs should so dwell, therefore he had a right to pray as he now did, "Make good thy promises, oh God. We have sore need of thy sheltering wings; enfold this dear child." Little wonder the prayer died down in sobs, and remained unfinished. Ah, well; He knew. Have little fear, brave girl, the sheltering wings will cover thee and the Everlasting arms will be underneath.

A few hours later she was gone, gone with her cheery ways, her sweet voice and her sunny presence. Asbury accompanied her as far as New York. Had the journey been a quarter of a century later they would of course have sailed from a western port, but arrangements had been made that she should sail with an English party from Liverpool.

A week later, in one of the largest churches of New York, a "farewell meeting" was announced for some outgoing missionaries who were about to sail. The hour was filled with prayer and testimony and songs of praise. The missionaries had mostly spoken of their interest in the work and how willingly they had given themselves to the cause, but the audience was chiefly interested in a young girl especially gifted who was leaving, so it was said, a loving home circle, having consecrated her life to this work.

Anticipating the natural wish of the audience to hear her, the kindly presiding officer, bending over, spoke a few words in her ear. She arose, stood a moment, and then the wondrously rich voice began in song "Nearer my God to Thee," with the words,

> "E'en though it be a cross that raiseth me,
>   Still, still my song shall be,
> Nearer my God to Thee;
>   Nearer to Thee."

The audience was moved to tears. Yet none of them guessed the story of the cross which had

brought the singer so wondrously near the Divine
One.

*   *   *   *   *

"Did you see that strange, poorly clad woman in
the rear of the church?" said one to another as
they slowly wended their way homeward after the
services, "That one who seemed to be so much
affected with Miss Stevenson's song." "Yes."
"No, she was just some one dropped in off the
street."

Later the bell rang at the home where Louise
was stopping with her dear friend Emma, who
had come to see her sail, and a poorly clad woman,
carrying a baby, asked to see Miss Stevenson.
Louise went at once to the room, where she was
waiting, and after eagerly scanning the visitor's
face, with a start of surprise, cried out, "Therese
Newton!"

Yes, it was she. In some way the poor, home-
sick, unhappy child had heard of the meeting and
of Louise, and she had yielded to an irresistible
desire to see her. She had not expected to make
herself known, but the song had broken up the
fountains of her heart and she had been impelled to
seek her out. Nor did she even now expect to
whisper aught of the sadly humiliated life she was
living, nor to speak of the cruel treatment of him
for whom she had left home and friends, who failing to realize the money he had expected, vented
his ill will upon the innocent, foolish young girl.

But before she knew it Louise had taken the
puny creeping babe in her arms, the young mother
had pillowed her head on her shoulder and was sobbing out the whole story.

"But you must go home." "Oh, Louise, I cannot go back. I must live out my wretched, miserable life. I have sinned away every opportunity of
my life. When I heard of my mother's death I
thought I would surely die, and I wanted, oh so
much, to go home, but he—" and she shuddered at
the name—"Oh, I dared not go."

"Then he was more angry than ever when we
heard of father's loss of property. No, I dare not
go," she moaned, "I believe he would follow me
and kill me."

And was this abject, cowering creature the old-
time happy, sprightly Therese?

Louise shuddered as she thought of the treatment she must have received to have brought her
to this.

"But you must go," she rejoined, and then
she told Therese of her father, of his solitary vigils in
the old home, and how as the weeks lengthened
into months his grief seemed to grow heavier.
Therese was greatly touched at the recital, and
amid her tears consented to make an attempt to
escape her present miseries. Perhaps, notwithstanding her grievous fault, there might yet be love
and a welcome in the shattered home.

That night Asbury Stevenson helped a scared

looking woman into a western bound train, and
placing a ticket in her hands bade her be of good
heart, yet she trembled each time a heavy footstep
passed through. Had she but known it she had
little need for fear. Even that morning the evil
man whose cupidity had wrecked her life, realizing
that the wealth he had expected to obtain through
her had slipped from his grasp, had put into
execution a plan long nurtured. He had sailed for
his own France; both mother and babe were
deserted.

The following morning as the missionary party
were being driven to the pier, Emma, who sat with
Louise's hand clasped in hers, said almost in a
whisper, " Louise, before you go I must—" We
lose the whispered story, if story it is, but catch
Louise's outspoken half deprecatory comment,
"Sly Asbury!" Whatever the communication was,
it must have been a pleasant one, for suddenly
Emma was gathered close in Louise's arms.

In a few hours the out-going party saw the
shores of their native land recede, and weeping,
waiting friends turned slowly about to gather up
again the broken threads of their busy lives.

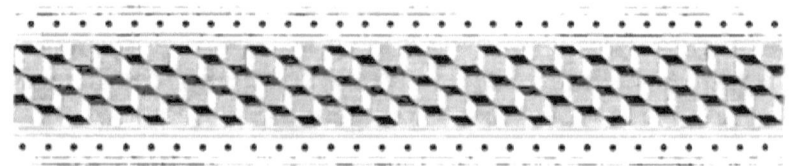

CHAPTER XX.

THERESE—ON BOTH SIDES OF AN OCEAN.

HE rapidity with which the events have shaped themselves has made it quite impossible to return to the stricken man whom we left by the grave of his beloved wife. Though Marie would gladly have had him come to her, yet he preferred to return to his own home, where during all this time he has lived in great loneliness. The greater part of the large house was shut up, the few rooms needed for his use being kept in order by a housekeeper. The only gleams of happiness that fell across his path in these dark days were when Marie's little Margaret would toddle to him, climb upon his knees, and in sweet baby fashion rub her little soft hand over his careworn face. At such times his face would light up, but the light would as quickly fade away. He seemed, as Louise had told Therese, to be settling into a hopeless melancholy.

His business had finally been "settled," which term by a strange misnomer has been chosen to indicate the final adjustment of property between a bankrupt and his creditors, and save for this house which had been the property of his wife, he was penniless. The peculiar misfortunes which had befallen him in his family affairs had brought him much sympathy, and when a new company opened the "mills" he was offered the position of manager, with a good salary.

Had he, like his old friend John Stevenson, had his family about him, he might with his rare business qualities, by steering clear of the rock of speculation, have yet done well,—but Margaret, the joy of his home, was gone. Therese, that blithe, bright girl who had nestled so close to his heart was, he felt sure, somewhere, perhaps in want of the necessities of life, paying the price of her folly.

Through the first months of his sorrow he had clung to Richard as his chief prop. How his heart had bounded as the telegraphic message, sent as soon as the result was known, told him of his oratorical victory. But all this died out as the miserable story of the evening's subsequent work reached him, and with the knowledge of his estrangement from Louise. He had seen him leave to seek his fortune in the West with but little hope that he would be able to withstand the temptations sure to be placed before him.

A few days after the burial of his wife an event occurred which did much to comfort him. This

was no less than a visit from John Stevenson.
Neither of the men said much, but there was that
in the hearty hand grasp which told the sorrowing
man that the past was forgiven, and that for him
there was no other feeling than that of genuine
sympathy. Indeed the Stevensons had come to
feel that the intention had never been wrong, but
rather that in the hopeless task of unraveling the
entanglements, hoping vainly that each week
would set matters right, their own little fortune had
gone down with his greater one.

But more appalling to them than loss of property
seemed the scattering of the family. Even the
death of Margaret they felt could have been borne
—alas, many a wife and mother has had to be lain
away—had the children all been present to comfort
and sustain the afflicted man. In comparison their
own lives seemed strangely full of blessings. So it
was with no feigned sympathy that John Stevenson
had gone to his old friend. Yet, even the sympathy of an old friend could not take the place of his
own, so after Richard's departure for the West he
had drawn entirely within himself, and with a growing chill at the heart his friends feared his mind
might give way under accumulation of sorrow.

Sometimes of a night, when the house was still,
he would wander aimlessly from room to room.
Unusually upon such a trip he would go to a drawer
where a few valuables were kept, open it, take from

its depths a laurel-crowned silver head, gaze fondly at it, and then with a sigh turn wearily away.

On one such night he was sitting gloomily by the fire which had been kindled in the grate, for the evening was chilly, the door bell now so seldom used, suddenly rang. Answering the summons himself, what was his surprise to see upon the doorstep a woman illy clad, with a wailing babe in her arms, and to hear a voice strangely familiar call out, "Father, father! I have come back to home and to you. You will not turn me away?"

It was Therese who had made the long journey back to the home from which she in her foolishness had fled.

What if her poor little life had been overshadowed by a mistake, so had his. With outstretched arms he welcomed her back to his desolate home, and Therese knew for the first time since her foolish marriage the value of the homely comforts of food and shelter.

It had not yet been two years since she had gone, but how she had aged. It seemed hardly possible that this haggard, worn woman could be identical with the merry, fun-loving girl who had danced through these great halls.

When her return became known Ruth Stevenson soon sought her, and to her, for the sake of the sweet friendship of other days, reticent as she might be to a curious world, Therese told her sad story, and in this tender and sympathetic friend she came to find her greatest comfort.

Before Louise sailed, she had found time for a hurried letter to Ruth. Referring to Therese she said, "We must remember that she has been more sinned against than sinning. It is not ours to judge harshly, and looking back now over the years it seems that the events that have so crushed her and others as well, were but the inexorable reaping of the careless sowing of other days. Be it yours, dear Ruth, to lead her back to happiness and a Christian faith. Remember she is scarcely yet a woman in years. Life may hold much for her yet." Thus the gentle ministry of love began which we must leave to the years.

Strangely enough it was left to Louise to be the bearer of a message that, though startling in itself, brought in reality the first breath of freedom which Therese had known since the miserable night of her flight. The message told of the death of her husband. He had died on shipboard. There was not the possibility of a mistake. A ship from America was being held in quarantine owing to the death of several of its passengers. In the printed list of the dead was the name of "Monsieur Martin Les Page, of New York, returning to France after an absence of years." Therese was free.

A few weeks later a little grave was made by

the side of Mrs. Newton's, and the young mother grieved anew for a little life gone out.

*   *   *   *   *   *

During all these weeks of intense feeling in their own home circle, the Stevensons had also been keenly alive to an event of great importance about occurring in what they were pleased to call "their home church" in Burton. This event appealed most strongly to all such who had worshiped years ago in the little log house. Not only had that been outgrown as we have seen, but also the "frame" structure which superseded it, and now a really elegant "stone," with all the modern conveniences of lecture, Sunday school and class rooms stood ready for dedication. And more, Dr. Blank, an editor who was well known to this people by the tempting dish of mental viands which he weekly served, was to preach the dedicatory sermon. There were many homes in Burton that would gladly have opened to the honored guest, but as it happened, this editor knew of the brave young girl who but so lately had gone from the Stevenson home, and had met and talked with the son who was preparing himself for his chosen life work. What more natural than that he should desire to know the father and mother. He proved an eloquent preacher in the pulpit, and a sharp student of human nature in the home. Indeed he had really entered this home as a searcher after a *cause*. He had seen the effect in the two young lives just mentioned. "Did some unsuspected talent", he asked himself, "exist in this plain father and mother, which perhaps being smothered by the meagre educational facilities of their early life had reappeared in their children?" but he had not been in the home a day, till he thought he had discovered the secret. The book shelves between the flower-filled windows had gently whispered in his ear, calling his attention to the well selected volumes with which they were filled. Glancing the titles over he found they had been culled from every realm, and touched upon every topic vital to the interest of a soul, and each book bore the marks of careful reading.

From his first entrance into the home he had been strongly attracted toward Edward, and thinking to push the acquaintance with the shy, reticent lad, he suggested a drive over the prairie. Under such circumstances the acquaintance progressed rapidly, for as the shyness wore off Edward proved himself so well informed, and withal such a good conversationalist, that the genial editor began to feel as though he was in company with one of his compeers rather than a country lad. Just as they were nearing the edge of a bit of woodland Edward suddenly drew rein and unceremoniously handing the lines to his companion, sprang out and began at once to carefully remove from the soil a plant growing by the roadside. Lovingly he brought his treasure back. "It is," said he in explanation, "a good specimen of the Lymegrass. I needed just this to make my collection of grasses complete for this locality."

Now if Dr. Blank had one hobby above another, it was the study of plant life, and these two, under the influence of this new bond, soon became fast friends, the Doctor waxing eloquent in the discussion of his favorite theme, aud the boy listening as under a spell, and when the next day the guest was leaving he quietly wrote in his private reference book the name of his young friend, Edward Stevenson.

Thanks to Louise's tact and influence John at the opening of the year was ready and glad to join Ruth and Edward in the Academy, but practical as of old, he insisted on "picking" his studies and laughed to scorn the suggestion of such studies as he deemed of little use in the actual battles of life.

"Baby Rose" was a baby no longer, but was fast becoming her mother's chief helper. She was a quiet home loving child, very like her brother John in appearance. When people saw her they were apt to say, "She will make a sensible, practical woman," and noticing her deft movements would be inclined to say that some day in a home of her own she would find her sweetest joy. She is not destined to thrill the world with her music, but like her sister Ruth, her voice and touch chord wonderfully well with the simple home tunes, and hearing her, her father vaguely recalls his own mother who is but a shadow of memory. So strangely are voice and form, yes, and mind and soul characteristics handed down from one generation to another. Perhaps of all the family none grieved so much as she for Louise.

She was not old enough as were the others to comfort herself with the nobleness of the action, nor yet to realize how much good she would do across the sea. She had been so proud of her when she had come home from the college, and listened wonderingly at the rare sweet music of her voice, her private opinion being that the angels made no such music. And now she was gone, gone out of her life forever, and the loyal little heart refused to be comforted. Before her going Louise had taken her in her arms and told her of the many homeless little girls whom she was going to work for, but no matter how dark she painted the picture the result was the same. Rose clung almost wildly to the sweet sister who was going.

Indeed the home hearts all ached. They were happy in the thought of her usefulness, but that illy took the place of the sunny living presence.

As soon as it had time to reach them a letter came which depicted the life so plainly, and was so rich in expressions of love, that with its reading the absent one seemed nearer.

Perhaps we cannot do better than to look in on the writer.

The long, wearisome ocean journey was at last

ended. The missionary party consisted of Mr. Winters and his bride and the English stranger. "It was a good thing," Louise wrote, "that these last were of the party, for the Winters were so dreadfully absorbed in each other she might as well have been sailing in another ocean." A mission was already started in the city of Foochow and they were to go there, stay awhile, get an inkling of the language, and then push on to the interior province which was to be their work.

Had it not been for that wonderful "something" that years ago at the plain altar of the little home church, had come in and wondrously filled this young heart, her soul must have fainted within her as she first looked upon the unspeakable degradation of those she had come to help. As she went through the narrow, reeking streets hunting for days for a lodging place, and for weeks for a room however small to begin the school, she began to experience the trial of her faith, but there is One who has promised "He will never leave nor forsake His children," and in those dark early days of her missionary life she wonderfully verified the promise. After a time she learned the language sufficiently to be able to tell the simple "old story," but it was not always possible to get listeners.

One day a miserable creature, a woman, had pushed her out of the room where she had gone to talk with her. About the door swarmed a crowd of dirty children. Suddenly the misery and

15

wretchedness of it all swept through her mind, and
yet, Christ died for these ; and His gospel if
allowed to come into these lives would uplift them,
cleanse not only their souls but their polluted bodies
as well. With a yearning perhaps akin to that of
the Master when He wept over Jerusalem, this
brave young girl longed to help these wretched
ones into a better life. As she paused, suddenly
the words and music of a home Sunday school
hymn came into her mind, and scarcely conscious
of what she did that sweet, rich voice that had in
other days held entranced the most cultured audiences, rang out on the stifling hot air. The little
children stopped their play, wretched women
peered out from the doorway of what they called
home, laborers stopped in the narrow, dirty street
and many followed the "foreign lady" to hear her
sing.

No need afterwards to hunt an audience, for the
audiences sought the singer. And yet in the home
land there had been those who had grieved over
this buried talent.

About the time that commencement roses had
again begun to bloom in the college campus, rich in
associations to both Asbury and Louise, a little
room in the most crowded part of that great
Chinese city had been obtained, and Louise as the
teacher of five little Chinese girls felt her life work
had begun. The Girls' College of Interior China
had been founded.   ·

CHAPTER XXI.

SOME GRADUATES—A WEDDING.

THE same June that witnessed the planting of the "Mustard Seed" across the ocean was unusually fraught with interest to the Stevenson home. In the very first weeks Edward and Ruth went out from the halls of the home Academy, and it was conceded that among all the long list of honorable alumni which this growing institution was beginning to boast, there had not gone out more thorough students than this brother and sister. The future plan was that these both should both in the Fall attend the college. Asbury was just leaving.

While their graduation was of great interest to the home, yet it was overshadowed by something that had lately been whispered about in connection with the closing days of Asbury's school life.

About the last of June he would receive the bit of parchment, the visible sign of that for which he had been striving. Then instead of coming at once westward, he was to make the journey East, and in the same rich old church where perhaps the echoes of his sister's voice still lingered, Louise's dearest friend Emma was to become his wife.

These were busy days for both Rachel and Ruth. There were so many tidying touches to be given here and there before the sweet young bride should arrive, and it was little wonder that as they worked, often the tears would fall as they thought of the absent one who far away, amid surroundings they felt sure their home eyes could not picture, had in a manner died to the joys of the home.

"Oh yes," thought Rachel, "if Louise were only here, she in her own peculiar way would lend a charm to the humble home." It must not be thought this mother gave her eldest daughter grudgingly to the Lord's service. No, she would not have uttered the words that would have held her back, but the mother heart ached, and sometimes the mother arms seemed unconsciously to again clasp this loved one to her breast, and perhaps after all, He who planted the mother love did not think less of the sacrifice because it was offered amid the throes of an aching heart.

The morning of their expected arrival at last dawned clear and bright. The little cottage really wore quite a holiday air. Surveying her finished work, practical Ruth gave the keynote to the family feeling when she said, "We may do what we will, and our home never be anything like the home Emma is leaving, and the most we can do is

to be our own true selves and give her a hearty
welcome." And they did, and Emma, child of the
city as she was, thought in all her life she had seen
nothing so beautiful as the cheery home room with
its flutter of white curtains and odor of home-grown
flowers.

Emma was her old sprightly self. Not a few of
her city friends had drawn sombre shaded pictures
of the privations that would be hers as the wife of
a western itinerant. To all this banter she replied
in the same vein, adding she had nothing to fear.
Had she not run the entire gamut of economy during the days of her club life, and if everything else
failed, she had understood that the West was noted
for its *fine potatoes.*

Yes, she was going willingly to share, as the
future might prove, the joys or sorrows, triumphs
or failures of this young student. After all we
opine that there will be but few failures.

Asbury is a close student. He has strong convictions of right and wrong. Aside from his collegiate education, his whole home life has been one
long school, in which the lessons of loyalty and
devotion to the church, as well as intelligence concerning her history and scope, have been well
learned. Moreover, the "fathers" say, he can
"preach." His chosen companion has both graces
of mind and of person, besides, too, her natural
sprightliness of disposition offsets well the sterner
gravity of his nature.

One thing time can never touch or efface, and that is the deep, invincible hatred which she has in her heart towards that great evil which in our modern times is like the fabled gorgon living by devouring our young men. Along with this hatred born as we know of a bitter experience, is a tender, pitying love for the victims. It will not be surprising if the future holds some special work along this line for her.

They are to go at once to a far western state and amid scenes new to each are to begin the solving of their own life problem. How happy they are! How many lofty dreams for the future! The college orations have been so full of such flowery terms as "whitened fields," "awaiting the sickle," and such like, that they imagine the future as a smiling goddess coming more than half way to meet them, her arms full of bundles labled "Success." Well, they are young! We who are older may smile, knowing well that time will brush away many of these illusions, yet we would not have youth one whit less hopeful.

Among the guests who came to do honor to the wedding occasion was Earnest Warren, Asbury's dearest friend during all his collegiate years. He found the sweet home life of the cottage very attractive. He has yet another year in college, and Ruth, too, expects to begin in September. We should not be a bit surprised if——.

On the morning of the departure of Asbury and

his young wife, Edward was surprised to receive a
communication which showed his honored friend,
the editor, had not forgotten him. There was an
expedition which an association of scientists were
sending out, made up of two or three professors
from so many colleges, whose object was to classify
and study the flora of certain parts of the North-
west. He had asked for and obtained a place on
the expedition for Edward. He well knew how
much this would mean to the boy, not only the
association with the learned men, but an opportunity to push his studies in plant life.

Indeed, nothing would have pleased this staid,
gray haired man himself, better than to have joined
the expedition and taken the tramp with the party,
but how could he, with his great, clamorous, "reading family" who would never have consented that
their mental purveyor should have gone off junket-
ing and left them to fare as best they might, but he
felt a real boyish thrill as he sent the welcome news
to Edward.

And Edward ; if he had suddenly stumbled upon
the pot of gold which tradition has assigned to the
end of the rainbow, he could not have been more
surprised and delighted. Being the "boy" of the
party, he was assigned certain chores, which if
done paid all expenses, and allowed him time for
the prosecution of his favorite study. Within a
week after the receipt of the letter he had completed his arrangements and was off.

How strangely still the house was during all that
summer ; only three children left of the old romping noisy half dozen, and of these three John and
Rachel could not hope that Time would spare them
much longer, for like a hurrying stream it was
bearing them rapidly to the responsibilities of life.
During this Summer Ruth and Rose greatly
relieved the mother of the cares of the house, while
John the younger became almost the sole manager
of the "store."   There had never been a regret
over this last venture.   It provided an income sufficient for the needs of the family.   The home was
not yet their own but the future seemed hopeful.

Relieved of care, the father and mother began to
find time for a renewal of the old companionship
which during the busy days of the last few years
had been largely lost in mutal anxiety for the welfare of their children.   It came to be a very usual
sight for them to be seen sitting either in the
shadow of the vine-covered porch, or under the
heavy boughs of the maple in the back yard.

Once as William Newton went by hurriedly he
saw them thus.   A bitter wave of feeling swept
over him.   Why was his home so desolate, his
beautiful wife gone, and his son, the idol of his
heart, a wanderer?   He knew that as this contented pair talked together more than likely their
conversation was of their children who bid fair to
be the crown of their old age.   But his heart
answered his question.   The Creator of each could

not be charged with partiality. Centuries before
the warning had been sounded, " Whatsoever a
man soweth, that shall he also reap."

" Yes," he bitterly acknowledged to himself, "We
were wrong, all wrong, from beginning to end; and
they of the farm were right. Life should mean
more than a struggle for riches, and there are pleasures more real, more lasting than are those which
appeal to the senses or upon which "Society"
stamps her approval.

The quiet Summer afforded an opportunity, too,
for Ruth and Therese to get their friendship back
upon the grounds of loving comradeship.

Poor Therese; it took many loving words from
Ruth to convince her that her life was not irretriev-
ably ruined. She could readily see her coming had
been a blessing to her father, for though the home
could never again take on its own cheery air, yet it
was growing brighter. The human heart hungers
for its own, and William Newton found his life happier as the strangely quiet woman who had come
back to him in place of the old gay, romping
Therese, went about the rooms, giving them here
and there a home touch. Thus far as she recognized her usefulness to her father she was glad,
otherwise she was wont to say she better never
have lived. Her sister Marie, conscious of her own
upright life, the honored wife of one of Burton's
wealthiest young men, happy in her own home,
proud of her two sweet little children, had not met

this young sister with outstretched arms; indeed there was that in her haughty manner which always reminded Therese of her disgrace. She had put on the heaviest mourning for "poor mamma," had felt shocked over "papa's failure," and now to have Therese come straggling in and bring the matter back fresh into the minds of all seemed too much. Better, much better would it have been, she thought, if Therese had born her troubles in silence. Let us not judge of her harshly, she was only a selfish society woman, eager for the praise of her little world, as vapid as herself.

"No, no, Ruth," Therese was saying as she and Ruth talked together "You know all about it. I cannot undo the past, my life is ruined. I am really fit for nothing. I have no education; I have learned a little smattering of several things, but I know nothing thoroughly. I never learned even to do housework as did you. For such a person I see now all too clearly there is no place in all this busy world. Even if it were not for my miserable marriage, I should have to write "failure" over my life."

And the hopeless manner in which she folded her arms and looked over toward the gleaming stones in the not far distant cemetery spoke more eloquently than could words of the despair she felt in her heart.

Ruth had no words for reply, but she gently kissed her and said as she was leaving, "You may feel thus now, but nevertheless I am sure there is a future for you, and in it you will find your work and your happiness; and in the years to come you will look upon these unhappy years as a dream."

That evening Ruth gave the substance of the conversation to her mother. Rachel was lost in thought for a time. Finally she said, "Therese is right in one thing. She has not sufficient education for a successful life. I do not mean the mere knowledge one gains from text books, for there are those whom circumstances have kept from the schools who by perseverance have largely made up for this lack and have given themselves a broader and truer outlook of life. Something of this kind is what Therese needs, something that will lift her out of herself. Do you remember the strategy Louise used to interest John, and how thankful we all are of the result?"

We cannot stop to detail the steps with which Ruth began at once to bring about this result. She carefully selected the books she hoped would interest Therese, and read her paragraphs from them. All this judiciously that she might not suspect her design. Finally, when she thought the time ripe, she suggested a home course of study, this under cover of a desire to review some of her own studies, and before Therese realized it the horror of the old life was slipping away and her active young brain was awakening to the interests of the great throbbing world, which from the days of Adam has ever found a place for each earnest

worker that has knocked at its portals. Aside from
the educational need, Ruth felt sure Therese would
never fully drop her burdens till they were lost in a
living Christian faith. Here again if she would be
successful she dared not be obtrusive, but before
the summer ended a slight, shrinking little figure,
heavily clad in black, was found each Sabbath by
Ruth's side in the Stevenson pew, and to the
gentle ministry of this young Christian who years
ago, in the little log church, had found how sweet
it was to lose her life in His, we may safely leave
for a time this childhood friend, trusting her to
impart something of her own simple faith.

CHAPTER XXII.

SEPTEMBER—A LETTER.

SEPTEMBER is always a busy month. During its days the summer idlers, as well as the summer resters return, the one to listen again to the alluring yet wearying calls of society, the other to take up the burdens of life afresh in the office, the pulpit or at the desk.

The schoolhouses that during the hot, dusty months have stood with their doors closed now have them flung wide open, and from all over the land in country, town and city, a long procession of little feet take up the march and in a twinkling these empty, gaunt, sentinel-like buildings wearing an hour ago an air of complete desertion, are teeming with life.

The quickening life blood, too, pulsates through the great halls of the colleges, and homes are yielding to them their choicest treasures. If it were possible they would gladly retain them longer; but no, there is nothing so necessary as that they be prepared for the inevitable future. So they bid them Godspeed, sending as a charge to the college that receives them this message from the poet king: "See to it that our sons may be as plants grown up in their youth; that our daughters may be as corner-stones, polished after the similitude of a palace."

Edward Stevenson returned from his summer jaunt of work and pleasure as rugged and brown as though he had been harvesting on the old farm acres. These weeks had meant much to him, much in the everyday association with men of education and culture. He had also been a careful student, and had often surprised the other members of the party by his accurate knowledge of plant habits. During the summer he was of great use in classifying and arranging the flora of the localities they studied, and in addition brought home a really excellent collection of his own. Something else happened, which because of its bearing upon his future deserves mention. This was the publication of his first article. His editor friend had said to him, "now if this jaunt has any interesting incidents that you think would read well, write them up and send them to me. I won't promise to publish, but you know," with that twinkle of the eye Edward had come to know, "we are always after the *best*."

To Edward the whole seemed full of interest, so he wrote up a modest little account of a few days' work, naming his brain child "After some Flowers," and in course of time it was published. He

managed to live through the sensation of first
seeing it in print, and (though he would never have
supposed it) life went on quite as usual. Of course
Mother Rachel read it, and like another mother
as she thought of his future, "she kept these things
and pondered them in her heart."

But now he was home; yes, and his belongings,
as were Ruth's, were packed, and as Asbury and
Louise had gone years ago, so these were going to
the same college. How vividly that other September came back, as with a hurried benediction and
prayer these two left the home.

Rachel had been called to the gate by the depart-
ing party to answer a question. As she started to
return to the house a sharp gust of wind rattled the
great tree by the path and blew from its branches
a nest which in the Spring had been a perpetual
source of delight, with its wealth of young bird
life. " Ah, well; perhaps it is only natural," thought
Rachel through her tears, "that young birds should
fly, but how desolate they leave the nest."

And desolate indeed seemed the home. It was
useless to put on a mask and feign a cheerfulness
neither parent felt. Yes, the young birds were
flying, and with them much of the cheer of the
home life. Edward and Ruth had left in the morning, and as they gathered about the small table for
the noon meal the mother broke down, and gave
up trying to hide her sense of loss. As she lay on
the couch in the living room her youngest son said,

"Mother, don't grieve. You have at least one child who will remain at home. I never intend to leave." "Nor I," chimed in Rose, and they kept their word.

John had yet another year in the academy. The last few months had witnessed a wonderful change in the sun-browned boy of the farm. He was not the same pattern with his ministerial brother Asbury, nor yet of the closer student Edward, but in his own practical way was likely to be as useful as either.

The boys and girls of this family were all of good physique, well formed and with suppleness of grace that indicates the sensibly reared family of young people. This was particularly true of John. He was a great tall, broad-shouldered fellow with dark eyes and hair to match. The latter with its soft wavy, curl would have been the envy of a modern belle. His voice was very like his father's, with a gentle cadence that made it peculiarly acceptable either in sickness or anxiety, and his touch was as gentle as a woman's. Like Louise, he had always been particularly helpful, indoors as well as out. About every home there are always numberless little "turns" by which, if willing to do them, a man can wonderfully lighten the household cares. Those in the Stevenson home came naturally to be left for John. It was understood when this last academic year was finished he would assume the entire management of the "store."

He was fast becoming of great use in the church, though naturally shy. As the result of a conversation with Louise before her going he had begun using his talents, and was developing as only young Christians can who do this, yet his practical views of life were shown here as elsewhere. About a year before this he had heard a sermon on "giving" which greatly impressed him. As a result he resolved to keep a careful account of his expenses and "pay over," as he termed it, the tenth. When the question of finances came up in the church his views were always so correct that unconsciously these matters came to be left more and more to him, and though the problem of church finances was often perplexing, yet he came nearer its solution than any one else.

While we have been lingering thus long, taking a final peep at the home that has so interested us, the students have been adjusting themselves to the year's work.

They did not enter the college as strangers, for their elder brother and sister had left a fragrant memory, and they were not long in finding their own niche in this busy hive of workers.

Edward's tastes inclined him to pay special heed to the sciences. As for Ruth, she continued the same thorough, painstaking student the home academy had known.

This year, with its routine of study, proved une-

16

ventful, but was none the less successful on that account.

The latter part of the winter was remarkable for a religious awakening, which spread until nearly all of the several hundred students who were not already professing Christians were converted. None who went through these strange weeks could ever forget them. The "Fathers" might tell of the old-time campmeeting, with its rapturous shouts, and fervent amens, yet this more modern movement, having its birth and carried on amid those who were nothing if not cultured, was not vastly different. There was the old-time conviction of sin, and if one might judge from the radiant faces, there was the old-time realization of one's own personal acceptance.

During all these weeks Edward Stevenson was strangely wrought upon. For years he had never questioned his personal relationship to his Saviour, but his tastes and inclinations were quiet, and he had never taken an active part in the church, but now—perhaps it was the result of the wonderful prayer meetings among the young men, perhaps it was the influence of his favorite professor who made it a point to bring out and interest every young man within his reach (alas that in his college days Richard Newton had not known such a friend)—but whatever the cause, he suddenly developed genuine leadership, and until the close of the meetings his voice was constantly heard in prayer

and exhortation, so much so that a short time after
their close he was given a license to preach. When
this news was carried home his father and mother
could scarcely credit it. "No, I cannot take it in,"
was his mother's comment, "yet I should be glad if
this should prove his life work." But John said, "The
idea! if Edward should happen to have a book on
hands he was interested in, he would certainly forget any appointment to preach which he might
have."

Thus fraught with duties the weeks went by,
until the coming of June, when the home at Burton
again smiled a welcome to its student inmates.
Edward came home only for a brief visit, as he had
been offered work in an editorial office. This did
not promise to be nearly so interesting as his last
summer's jaunt, but though he little thought it, this
became the ground-work upon which his future
largely rested.

Before Ruth's return she wrote her parents that
she had something to tell them which she could
not write. They easily guessed her sweet secret,
and it took only a glance at the plain gold band
which she wore upon her return to confirm their sus-
picion. This had been Earnest Warren's last year in
college. It was little wonder that he desired to win
for himself this young girl whose gentle, gracious
ways, as he had seen, had made her presence in her
father's home a benediction. He had expected to
enter the ministry, but he had been offered a posi-

tion as teacher in a young college. This seemed to suit his present inclination and it was arranged that in a year or two he would claim his bride.

The memory of Ruth's successful school term still lingered in the home neighborhood, so much so that she was offered a position as one of the teachers in the home academy. She finally reluctantly concluded to forego another collegiate year, yet she did not mean her education to cease, for she began a course of home study and pursued it unweariedly.

Very often at this time the thoughts of both Ruth and her mother turned with a new tenderness to that brave one so many miles away. Until now Ruth had not realized what the anguish of Louise must have been when she had seen *her* happiness shipwrecked, but this realization began to dawn upon her, when in answer to a letter telling of her new-found happiness and plans there had at once come one from Louise breathing earnest wishes for the continuance of her happiness. Although she spoke hopefully of her work, and wrote touchingly of the degradation about her, yet amid it all there was an undertone of sadness, as if the writer had looked into the coffin of a dead joy, and this the mother recognizing and yearned afresh for the blithe "singing bird" of the home, but she said in her heart, "She did right; yes she did right." But alas! for the pity of it!

CHAPTER XXIII.

A KANSAS PREACHER—HIS WORK.

IF ONE who happened to be of a speculative turn of mind had chanced to find himself on a certain western-bound passenger train one day two summers before the events of the last chapters he would have looked with considerable interest upon a young pair who seemed very much at home amid their surroundings. There was about each a quiet, well bred air, and a something that proclaimed them fresh from their books. In addition to this there was also an air of—well, if not exactly self-complacency, at least of self-satisfaction. Further, if the onlooker, bearing the proper credentials in his face, had with the freedom of travelers engaged the young man in conversation he would have learned that the pair in whom he was interested was the Rev. Asbury Stevenson and wife, late of an eastern college, that during the last weeks of the college year a presiding elder of one of the frontier districts in Kansas had written the faculty to name a young man who could take

charge of a small "station" (considerable emphasis
on that word) on his district, "where the principal
work would be to build up the charge, even to the
church building itself," and from that correspondence
had come this journey. Their destination was
Falls City which city the young divine explained
took its name from being built upon a river by that
name.

"Ahem, and have you ever built a church?
Know anything about it?" the interrogator might
have asked.

"No, but—" Here the Rev. Mr. Stevenson
would have paused, and in some inexplicable way
one would have gotten the impression that half a
dozen such undertakings would be a matter of
small importance to this brave youth.

We too will watch these young travelers awhile.
In a little while their train has reached that young
stripling of a city which to the traveler seems only
the place where all the inhabitants of the nation are
all at once engaged in the frantic effort to change
cars and make no mistake, but which the native res-
idents tell us is really one of the finest cities in the
world, hence call it *Kansas* City. Here two alterna-
tives were offered: they might continue their journey westward at once, on a freight car, or they
might remain until morning and take a passenger.
Life thus far had held no freight car experiences so
they continued their journey at once, and as a
result of their decision continued it for many long

wearisome hours, even until they of the later passenger had jauntily passed them by.

They were to go to a young city (they had left the *towns* all *east* of the Mississippi) west of Topeka, and thence south fifty miles in a stage.

"The whole country looks as if it were not finished," was Mrs. Asbury's comment as she peered out of the car window. And so it did. There were miles and miles of green prairie, with not a single trace of a living being. The sun beat down remorselessly, without a tree in sight. Occasionally there would be a little cluster of unpainted box like houses that stood upon the prairie, with the tall grass growing, quite up to the doors.

At last the railway part of the journey came to an end, and as the Rev. Asbury was leaving the freight he looked rather lugubrious as he did some careful brushing of his lovely "silk tile." But the real pleasure began .with the stage ride. Such beauty! The grass was so green! and was as soft as any of Mrs. Ward's elegant carpets. One novel feature was the undulating swells of the prairies, which were not unlike the waves of the ocean. Here and there great herds of cattle pastured, and oh, the flowers! They were of every form and hue, and before the journey was half completed both of the young people were in love with their adopted state.

"It seems to me it is rather a windy day," remarked Emma as she drew her wrap about her. The driver smiled and murmured something about

"Kansas zephyrs;" which phrase she grew to know more about later on. A little purple cloud lay very innocently in the western sky, upon perceiving which Asbury noticed that the driver whipped up his ponies and kept them at a break-neck pace, eyeing the cloud in the meanwhile.

At last in a relieved tone he exclaimed, "We'll make it!" Half an hour later they were clattering up the streets of what seemed a very tiny village that had lost itself in immeasurable distances. The wind was blowing quite a gale, but the driver managed to say, "There is our new court house; and there our school house." There was something in the very tone which implied expected admiration, but it was now growing dark rapidly. As the travelers started to go from the stage to the hotel a great wind lifted the elegant "tile" from the head of the Rev. Asbury and sent it whirling down the street. It was useless to follow it, though he half started to do so. Afterwards he called this his first "Concession," for the next morning he purchased a regulation broad-brimmed "slouch," and it was many a day before he owned a counterpart of the first.

They were barely housed when the rain was falling in torrents, and the thunder—nothing like it had ever been heard before. They afterwards learned this was a peculiarity of the climate. Nature was wont to act as if she had an extra amount of work which must be accomplished on schedule time. The rain would fall in torrents, thunder's crash, and lightning play in a most terrific manner, but in an hour the earth would be bright and smiling after her bath, and the roads as hard as a floor.

Early the next morning the young minister hunted up the "brethren," and preliminaries were arranged for getting to living. He and his young wife received a hearty greeting, and with each new presentation, before the conversation closed the invariable question was asked, "You have of course seen our new court house and school building?" and the tone implied that not to have done so and be able to admire was unpardonable. One of the first acts of the baby city had been to vote bonds, and utilizing the fine building stone that abounded in every hill, had built a really fine court house and school building which stood on the actual prairie, the pride of every man in the city, who looked upon them as the forerunners of the great city that was to be. They also served other purposes than those planned in the original. Done in lithographs, they tickled the fancy and unloosened the purses of eastern capitalists. Besides these, the town consisted of a business street and a few of the box-like houses they had noticed along the railway.

During the forenoon the Rev. Asbury with a volunteer guide, a member of his church, started with considerable expectancy to the site of the new church.   The letter describing the enterprise had read something like this: "We are not strong numerically, but the imperative need is a *church building*.   This we *must have* to hold our share of the incoming population.   Such an enterprise has been begun, but abandoned.   We have the finest site in the city.   The foundation is laid, a part of the building material is on the ground, and we must have an active young man to push the work."   It all sounded so well, and this ministerial fledgling started out fully expecting to find the workmen hammering away upon a building that would match the court house and school.

As the walk progressed, and house after house was left behind his anxiety increased.   Finally he struck what seemed the open prairie, but had he been familiar with the map of the city he would have known that he still was in its very heart.   At last his companion stopped, exclaiming "Here we are."   "Here is what?" Asbury asked.   "The church building."   Involuntarily he rubbed his eyes.   In front of him was a tall, rank mass of what seemed bushy weeds, which he had already learned was the native sunflower.   Peering through these, he saw that an excavation had been made and a few foundation stones placed in position.   From appearances it perhaps *had* been begun, and most certainly abandoned.   The "building material on hand" was represented by a pile of native stone, also sunflower over-grown.

"You have your subscriptions all right?" Asbury asked in a voice that sounded strange even to himself.

" Umph, that's what we sent for you for."

" Now, young man, do you think you can build this church?" and his interlocutor turned a critical look upon him, "because if you can't you had better take the first stage east."

Asbury did not answer, but on the walk back he did some hard thinking. Strangely enough, this was something even his young wife could not help him to decide. To sum it all up, he saw clearly what was expected of him. He was to preach twice each Sabbath, a formidable undertaking in itself, take a subscription of strangers, many of them not connected with any church, and personally superintend every detail of a work he knew nothing about.

As his chronicler I am glad to write that at this point what in the home neighborhood was known as the "sturdy common sense of the Stevensons" asserted itself. Things were not as he had expected, "but God helping him he would not fail." Sweeping through his mind came innumerable instances of which he had read, of the heroic efforts of others to plant the church elsewhere. Indeed was not his own sister meeting every day discouragements far greater than any that could confront him? He remembered how as he had sat about the glowing fire in the comfortable farm home, he had been thrilled as he had read of the heroic endurance of those who had braved Indian dangers on the frontier. It had all seemed so grand then, should he yield till every known means had been tried?

"*No*," and though the little handful who called themselves the "Church" little guessed it, their coveted new church was as truly built in that hour of introspection on the part of the young pastor as it was a year later when a delighted audience gathered to hear the dedicatory sermon.

At length a little house, very much of a pattern with the rest, was procured, and the home life begun. There were a few elegant "touches" from the old luxurious home of Emma, but after the last piece of the plain furniture was in place Emma exclaimed, " Now if Louise and I had only known it, Mrs. Hoyson's home was elegance itself." But what if it was plain? They were rich in love for each other, rich in hope for the future and in consecration of their young lives to the work.

Emma never forgot her first Sabbath. A kind of hall above one of the business houses was being used as a place of worship. By the side of it stood a one-story building which had been covered with a tin roof (lumber was a luxury to be used as sparingly as possible). She had never heard her young husband attempt to preach, and felt a wifely anxiety that he should favorably impress his hearers. The wind was sweeping down the street with a momentum that carried everything not securely fastened before it. During the service the tin roof beneath kept up a monotonous rise and fall with a harsh grating noise not unlike the wail of imprisoned spirits. As for the preacher himself he had gone to this service feeling entirely unable to meet it. He had never so realized his insufficiency before. As he arose to announce the hymn, and he beheld the questioning, critical, yet not unfriendly faces before him, a wild desire to flee through the door which stood invitingly open, seized him. But no, he half argued with himself, he could not be mistaken. That conversion of his, years before in the little room of the log house, had been a very real occurrence, yet none the less so than the subsequent still but persistent voice which had led him into the ministry. Clearly as though a voice had spoken came the promise, "Lo, I am with you." A sudden agonized prayer for help went up, and the sermon began. An hour afterwards he could not have told what he preached, whether the words were lame or otherwise, but certainly the Spirit inspired them. A strange awe fell upon the little assembly. Many had come in curiously for a glimpse of the "new preacher," but melted before his earnestness. At the close no less than five came forward to unite with the church.

The next morning he promptly began the work of obtaining subscriptions. Finally he had a sufficient amount to begin. The details of the various steps of this undertaking need not be recounted, but he soon found he must personally superintend each one. Besides, funds **were scarce,** and every dollar must **be** made to count, **and** so, though Emma remembering the stately and dignified Dr. Eloquent of the home church, winced a little as she saw her husband in working attire making a "hand," she at length grew reconciled to the new order of things.

There was one unexpected feature of the new life which charmed each, and that was the remarkable **general** intelligence of the people. It was no unusual thing to find rolled up and laid away **upon** one of the "general utility shelves" of the box houses a diploma bearing the seal of some good college, while its owner busied herself with the humbler duties of homekeeping. Men above the average **stood behind** the counters, or edited the "hustling" **newspapers, or doctored one** when the native malaria got **too** deep a hold.

The cosmopolitan character of the new home **was shown** in the fact that in a single afternoon **there** were callers whose homes from which none had been long away, had been in New York, Virginia, Ohio, and indeed nearly every state in the Union, was represented in the Sunday congregation.

The new church was to be of stone. Ten miles distant was a ridge of hills which took their name **from** a beautiful stone found there in great quan-

tities. This was to be used for the front and finish-
ing, and hither the young preacher took many a
trip where he lent a hand in the quarrying.

At last, after more than a year of hard work, the
building was completed, and a lovely Sabbath saw
its dedication. The deep "Italian" sky, in the language of the local poets, was never bluer than now.
The gentle "zephyrs" toned themselves down to
suit the occasion as they left the green sward of the
prairie, and perhaps there never was a happier congregation than that which gathered that day.

The young pastor, to whom all acknowledge is
due the present success of the enterprise, has lost
the "student air" and now would be known anywhere as the keenly alive, western "preacher."
He does not consider his work done with the com-
pletion of the building; he is now as keenly alive
to the spiritual upbuilding of his congregation.

Nor will this last prove a less easy task. Indeed,
no pastor either East or West will say that it ever is,
yet on the frontier it is especially hard. There is
the rush to become established in business, and the
temptation to forget God in the hurry is always
present. Besides vice takes on certain more em-
phatic forms, and happy the leader of a flock that
successfully copes with all these, yet in this last
work Asbury Stevenson will not stand alone, for in
the heart of his young wife is as strong a hatred of
sin as in his. So leaving them for a time, we bid
them God speed, and adieu.

CHAPTER XXIV.

A RETROSPECT—A WEDDING—DEATH OF RICHARD NEWTON.

IT HAS been many years, some wearisome, some joyous, since the group of watchers stood upon the brow of the hill at quaint, picturesque Lynton, and waved us a last adieu, as with the two happy pairs in the great canvas covered wagons we left its winding, shady street forever. We have since seen the terminus of that long journey, the then western wilds, develop and come to teem with life and a marvelous civilization.

It has been ours to see and note the struggles in the founding and guidance of the homes which were established, that May day in the village church at Lynton, and the working out of the individuals' problem of worldly prosperity.

In these two homes, as in every home, there has been constant sowing of seed, either good or bad. The harvest of some has already been garnered, but all seed does not ripen in a year, nor yet in a decade, and as the patient husbandman having seen to it that his seed possesses the true germinal principles of life, having planted them, leaves them in perfect faith to the sure offices of nature to effect the growth, and in its season with unerring sureness gather the harvest, so we, having watched this daily home sowing, sometimes with joy, as often with dread, must leave to the years the final gathering.

It will be ours therefore to drop the curtain, nor will it be raised until such a number of years has passed that the fruits of the home growing will be easily recognizable. We hold it yet a moment to note one or two events of interest to us.

The cottage home at Burton again wears a holiday appearance, and we find that Earnest Warren has come to claim his bride, and gentle Ruth Stevenson is to go out from the home forever. Her loss is going to fall heavily upon both father and mother, and as the preparation for the wedding festivities progress their hearts grow heavier, for from the time that her father had held her in his great strong arms, she a wee winsome babe, she had nestled very near his heart, indeed in many ways she was his own counter part. She had always been so unselfish in her life, an offset in many instances to the more impetuous nature of Louise and of her brothers. It was hard to imagine the home without her.

Yet there was much comfort in knowing that he who was to be her husband was so worthy. He had already won for himself an enviable name as a

teacher in the college to which he had gone when
his own school days had ceased. But he desired to
still further pursue certain branches of study. An
opportunity had offered itself for him to go abroad
for a year or two, and he desired that Ruth should
accompany him.

Ruth had been, as we know, loth to give up the
final years of her college course, but the home
needs had seemed to make imperative the acceptance of the position offered her in the Academy, so
it was with genuine pleasure she looked forward to
a year or two of further study with her husband, in
one of the cities of Germany.

The wedding day at length dawned. Asbury and
his young wife honored it by making it the occasion
of their first visit home. Their coming has been heralded for weeks, and there is an undertone of excitement which strikes us as very strange. John the
younger, proud of his commission, has driven to
fetch them from the train, and see, they are at the
gate! Ah, now the mystery is plain. Grandmother
Rachel is herself at the carriage, and her great
bearded boy has held her in his arms for an instant
as he gives her the greeting kiss, but she hardly
notices it, she is so eager and enwrapt with the
strange dainty bundle of white cambric and flannel
motherly Emma is handing out. Now they are in
the house, and oh, strange sight! When the little
face is uncovered and she bends to kiss it she suddenly breaks down, and as her own tears fall fast

no eye of all in the room is dry. Clasping the wondering babe to her breast she has sobbed aloud,
" Sweet, sweet baby Louise!" So has the absent
one been remembered.

The student Edward has also come from his
books.

The hours fly swiftly, and soon the event which
has summoned them is a thing of the past. And
Ruth is gone.

Asbury lingered for a few days' visit of course.
The pulpit of the new home church was offered
him, and old neighbors and interested friends who
had known him all his life gathered to hear him
preach.

Among them, hardly daring to look up, sat
father and mother Stevenson. There are some
things which can only be imagined, among such is
the quiet thrilling happiness which filled these faith_
ful hearts as they heard their first born " expound
unto them the things of God." But could this
strangely earnest, free, and at all times really eloquent young speaker be their own quiet, shy child?

Ah, brave hearts, it was yours in the years you
had not only him but his brothers and sisters as
well with you in the little plain log home, to lay the
foundations of the character each is developing.
You indeed builded better than you knew with
your own simple faith but there came a day when
your last moulding touch was given and you yielded
them to others. In your own humble lives you lit-

tle guessed the breadth of soul, the enlargement of vision that should come to each through the study and associations of their college life. And in the case of this your first born, within the last years God has been his teacher in the school of experience, and as you hear his burning words you may well say humbly, " What hath God wrought?"

A few days and the visitors are gone. Of the many that once gathered about the table but John and Rose are left, and the father says, " We must all love each other the more."

*   *   *   *   *

We hold the curtain yet a little longer, this time to catch a glimpse of a procession that with a sable hearse and nodding plumes slowly winds its way to the city of the dead. Before we join in its measured tread we shall have to take a glance westward.

Following the marriage of Ruth, Asbury had been back in his western pastorate perhaps about two years. These had been spent in hard work. Falls City was not a very promising field for a teacher of morality. It is true his beautiful church was a standing invitation to all who would to enter and worship, yet it took all the efforts of the watchful and alert young pastor to withstand the steady attacks of sin and vice which in the first years of every western town contended for mastery.

That plague spot of civilization, the open drink shop, flourished unrestrained by law. There would be days and nights when from the adjoining ranches, "cowboys" as those having charge of the great herds of cattle there were called, would gather in, drink, gamble, and hold a carnival of sin. At such times the terrified inhabitants could only close their doors and windows and listen in dread to the crack of the pistol which told of the summary settlement of some fancied insult.

Because of all this it was not with a great deal of surprise that on a morning following a "cowboy raid" Asbury received a hasty summons to visit a man who had been shot in some kind of a melee during the night and was said to be dying. Yet if the message gave him no surprise, a bit of information volunteered on the way did. It was to the effect that the wounded man had particularly asked for him by name. Who among all the wild men gathered there knew him?

Soon he was shown into a little, narrow, low room where lying upon a bed lay—could he believe his eyes—his once brilliant playmate and friend, Richard Newton.

Asbury Stevenson had learned something of his Master's tenderness during these years of trial. His old rigid notions had insensibly softened; he had been growing in these latter days to look beyond the sinner to the causes that made him such, and now Louise could not herself have knelt more tenderly than did he, nor could her touch have been gentler than was that of this elder brother of hers who was filled with ineffable pity as he beheld his old-time comrade.

The wounded man was still conscious. "No, he cannot live," said the physician, "nor will it hasten his end if he is carefully removed." This in answer to an anxious question of Asbury. In an hour Richard was lying in the cool little spare room of the parsonage, and Emma was ministering to his needs.

After intervals of pain, fragments of his story were gleaned, and piecing them together the Stevensons guessed the last few months had been full of dissipation, spent somewhere further West. There he had learned of Asbury's residence here, and a longing desire to look on them seized him. He had not yet fully decided whether or no he would make himself known, and had gone to the hotel. He had but lately lost his all at the gambling table, and that night he thought he saw his opportuity to win back a part of his loss. Somehow at the cards, he could not tell how, trouble had arisen, and he knew no more.

After he had told this much he sank into a stupor, from which nothing could arouse him. Sometime during the next day as Emma was performing some little office at the bedside, Baby Louise toddled up, and stooping to take her in her arms Emma called her by name. Suddenly the great dark eyes of the stranger opened, and lighted up with something of their old-time beauty, and bent a questioning look, first upon the child and then upon the mother. Divining his thought Emma bent and whispered:

" Yes, we named her for Louise."

A wistful look grew in the eyes, which Emma thought she understood, and bending she smoothed a place and laid the little Louise beside him. To her surprise the child did not shrink, but with her baby hands gently stroked his face. And thus he died.

Ah, little Louise, was it some subtle influence of whose laws we as yet know nothing, that coming from the great heart of her whose name you bear, caused this baby act that comforted the dying man? Who can tell?

" No, he must not lie in a western grave. With our going there will be none to bear him in remembrance. His body must lie by his mother's, at home." It was Emma who had spoken, as she with her husband stood over the lifeless clay which lay, with the old-time beauty restored in every feature.

"*And she*," and Asbury's voice grew very tender, and his eyes instinctively turned toward the Orient, "would not want him to go to his grave unattended."

In a few hours all that was mortal of Richard Newton was being carried eastward, and a solitary saddened man accompanied it. Very content was he in his humbleness to leave the spirit with the Great Judge who knoweth the soul environments of us all, and in his judgment has promised to remember that we are dust.

And it is this body we have seen borne to the grave. It had lain in the old home over night; but once was the covering removed. The watchers in the adjacent room were startled by the sound of footfalls. Quietly looking, they saw an old man, bent, yet not with the weight of years, go slowly to the bier, lift the lid and place therein a silver head. No, they could not be mistaken, for the delicate golden leaves of laurel glistened even in that dim light. Having placed it, he bent a moment over the still rarely beautiful face, and with a groan turned away.

A few weeks later another grave was made, and William Newton was no more. Poor Therese must have died under all these cruel blows had it not been for the Christian faith she had learned. But her future seemed indeed without a ray of promise. So at least it seemed to her, as in her sister's elegant room—it was impossible for her to remain alone in the great house—she sat rocking Marie's baby, William. Was there any use, after all, for her to try? She had tried, oh, so hard, and just when her own and her father's heart seemed knitting in the closest sympathy, these last trials had come, and now he, her last friend, was gone. No, it was no use to try.

Just then the door opened and the housemaid entered and handed her a letter. "It is from

Ruth," said she, as she broke the seal. Yes, it was from Ruth, who wrote such gracious, tender words of sympathy, that poor Therese wept as she had not during all these dreadful days. Then followed words of comfort. Who has not realized that there are times when the most comforting thought that can come is that " there is somebody else who cares." Finally came the glad news that they were to return shortly, and the half playful, half in earnest injunction to keep up her studies, and that Earnest was very sure he could find a place for her as teacher.

" And, mind, you are to live with us."

Wise Ruth; she knew Therese's surest means of happiness lay, as does every one's in work. A grief that folds its hands is soon well named despair, hence she sought, and did arouse her to action, for as she finished the letter she said with an air of decision, " No, I will not give up."

But our curtain refuses to remain longer, so we leave not only Therese, but all the others in whom we have grown interested, to the tender mercies of the years.

CHAPTER XXV.

A FAMILY REUNION—GATHERED THISTLES.

EIGHTEEN hundred and ninety-three! How much may happen in a decade; yet if we add to that, one, yet another, as we must since we last looked in upon our friends, the changes may be startling. If this is true of a family, it is none the less so of a nation.

With the rapid march of the years, almost the last trace, except in the hearts that still ache, of the dreadful war which threatened at one time to devastate both North and South, has been wiped out. During these years cities have been planted, or already existing as little more than villages, have grown with a rapidity that would startle even Aladdin himself.

The new forces of steam and electricity have revolutionized the commonest affairs of life. One can now whiz by on a car drawn as the ancients would have said, by magic or by a trick of the same conjurer, talk with a friend a thousand miles away, recognizing the very intonations and peculiar inflec-

tions of the voice; and yet staid history assures us
that this wonderful land which has show'n such a
marvelous capacity for development was but four
short centuries ago unknown to civilization, but at that
time an intrepid mariner sailed out from safety into
the unknown, and after a journey of which every
detail is now hunted and made much of, he was able
to lay at the feet of the old civilization this new
world, brimming over as he himself little guessed
with possibilities for the future.

Of course its great rivers were then as yet unknown, its great inland seas unsuspected, and its
cities unbuilt. Still its mere finding was a great
event, and therefore it is little wonder that the na-
tions of the earth, looking back through the centuries,
resolved to celebrate the anniversary of its finding,
and to do so, had arranged to bring the choicest pro-
ducts of their civilization and exhibit them on a scale
of magnificence hitherto unattempted. The winds
caught up the story of this coming splendor and
wafted it across meadow and hill, heather and
steppes. The current carried it beneath the waves
and whispered it to the dwellers in the region beyond,
and the eyes and thoughts of the world turned
America-ward.

Among the many little knots or groups, who
under their own sky and in their own tongue discussed the wonders that were to be seen by a
journey across the ocean, there is but one that
interests us.

In a well built mission house in one of the interior cities of China a little group of missionaries has lingered, evidently to talk over "something." A large company of comfortably and neatly clad girls have just marched out of the chapel, for the "mustard seed" has taken deep root, grown and spread itself not unlike its scriptural ancestor. Instead of the erstwhile narrow, dirty little room in a wretched part of the city, now on one of the choicest knolls, with grounds enough about them to give the inmates a breath of God's pure air, stands a cluster of buildings upon which they who planted in tears, look with genuine pride. Besides the comfortable home for the missionaries there is a roomy school building, in which is the chapel we have just seen. The dream of a "girls' college" is a reality.

Let us glance for a moment at the missionary group. Most of them are reinforcements from the home land, hence strangers to us, but we are at once attracted to a bright, happy—yes, happy, though it seems a happiness born of pain—face of a woman whose brown wavy hair is beginning to be thickly sprinkled with silver. She has left the organ over whose keys her fingers have been idly straying, and is joining the little group who are eagerly discussing some question. As she comes up one speaks, evidently for all, "No, we cannot all go, much as would like to, but one can be spared from the work, and that one must be our brave, cheery worker Louise, who in all these years has never been to the home land." "Yes, so say we all."

Louise Stevenson, for it is she, stands for a moment strangely disconcerted. For months they of the mission house have been reading of the wonderful happenings at home but better to each, than sight of sculptor's dream in marble, or of artists' sublimest conception, would be to look again into the dear faces at home, or to sit at the ingleside where mother was wont to hum a lullaby, and for weeks as the world's procession of travelers America-ward grew, this thought has taken root and grown at the mission house, "cannot at least one of us go?" And it was this they had lingered to discuss, and their decision we have heard.

At length Louise spoke, and her voice trembled. "Well, I don't want to seem selfish"—at this, they knowing her peculiarly unselfish life smiled—"but it seems strange that father and mother should still live. Sometimes it seems that I *must* see them again, and then I can contentedly return and—." But she did not finish the sentence with her voice, but involuntarily her eyes sought a little sacred spot visible from the chapel window, where during the years workers had one by one lain down to rest. So it was settled. Louise, the hard-working missionary, was going home, and an outgoing steamer carried the news homeward the very next day.

Again and again during all these long years she

had expected to go, but the needs had been so
urgent, and she had seemed so well adapted to the
work; besides her health had been good, while that
of other missionaries had failed and when they had
been ordered home for rest, she had always been able
to fill up the breach. And none knew better than the
group of missionaries in the chapel, indeed the
whole board of missions as well, who proudly
pointed to "Our college;" that its inception and its
steady march towards success was due to the clear
brain and indomitable perseverance of her who was
now to take her first vacation.

From that hour when she had held entranced with
her voice her first unclean, half-clothed audience, she
had known no rest. She had used her pen vigor-
ously, and in response welcome donations came in
for the proposed college. The fame of her voice
grew until it reached and captured the ear of many
of the better class. Nor was that her sole secret.
Her cheery face won friends, and her complete
self abnegation—indeed she seemed to have lost all
thought of self, and to be lost in her work—with her
instinctive sympathy and helpfulness won the hearts
of all who came in contact with her.

The peculiar rescue work of the mission sometimes uncovered such loathsome cases of misery
that occasionally one less brave than she would
shrink. Sometimes the girls who came to them
were little tiny tots who had come into the world
only to suffer at the hands of parents or friends.

Such Louise would take into her own arms, bathe and clothe.

And now she was going home! The news flew, and when the day came for her to sail she passed through long dusky ranks that had gathered to do her honor, but alas for overstrained nature, in the stress some of these forgot their studied parts and could only wail aloud in true oriental style.

*　　　*　　　*　　　*　　　*

As the ship bears Louise homeward we pause to gather up a few broken threads of the past.

"Louise is coming home!" With strangely blurred eyes an old man had sat down to read aloud the letter, bearing the strange foreign postmark they had come to know so well, and the first few lines he read told the story.

Grandmother Rachel was sitting in her easy chair by the windows of the "new rooms" she had planned so long ago. Her joy at hearing the glad announcement must be imagined. Later as she wiped her glasses she said, "and the other children must come too, and we will see them all together again before we go hence." But before that joyful gathering we shall have to ask why we find them sitting so contentedly in the old home.

Their youngest son had made good his boyish vow, registered over the glossy mane of his favorite "Beauty." Perhaps a rapid sketch of his life would not be amiss.

William Newton in his brightest days had not

possessed a greater desire to "get on in the world" than did this country boy, but there was this difference: The lad was God serving and God fearing, and as we have seen, in his earliest years began by rendering back unto God a part of all his gains, yet withal he possessed true business acuteness. He was greatly fascinated by Asbury's stories of western life, and resolved to visit that marvelous country at the earliest opportunity. He had a reason for this, he was not yet ready to share with anyone. That Arizona land haunted him like a nightmare. He had read and studied with interest everything that came in his way since he had had the "worthless deed" in his possession. Once he had read that copper had been found, yet not in quantities that would make its "reduction" profitable. " What if," and this was his own little dream that lightened many a homely task these days, "what if this particular bit of land should possess the valued metal." Therefore he could scarcely conceal his satisfaction when one July morning found him journeying west, with a whole month at his disposal. Once in Asbury's home he was not long in making his plans known, and a week later he had started on a tour of personal inspection.

The land was easily located. Instead of being a part of a continuous plain as he had supposed, he found it broken, with here and there great rocky fissures, and not greatly distant from the mountains.

He did not fail to feel the pulse of local opinion concerning its value. "Arid," "worthless," the precise terms used by the lawyer years ago, and his own observations as he wearily tramped over it, confirmed the verdict.

The old scene in the lawyer's office came back to him, and though he could not have explained why, he experienced a new sense of loss. Until now he had not guessed how much he had builded upon these acres. In his tramp he had neared a gulch, and being wearied in body he sat down upon a ledge of rock, and sitting there gave vent to the disappointment he could not but feel.

"How useless this part of creation, anyway." That mountain over there he had been told contained not only copper, as he had read, but metals even more precious, but worthless, all because that homely necessity, coal, had to be brought from such a distance.

"But what is that?" As he half lay, half sat, he had been mechanically kicking at an unoffending stone that lay a little looser than its fellows. Instantly his old lessons in geology with Louise flashed upon him. "I believe that is a surface indication of coal!" What if it were? His heart bounded, for that very morning he had been told how profitable copper mining would be, if there were only coal.

He examined more closely, then returned to his stopping place, and later returned with pick and

18

shovel, and soon became convinced of the proximity of coal. How much he did not know, this he left for those of more experience.

He anxiously watched the workers for the next two days, and heard almost as an echo of one of his dreams, " It is a good paying vein!"

The news spread. With characteristic western push a company was formed and within a week he had received an offer that equaled in value the old home farm.

John suddenly lost all interest in a further western trip, and hastened home with the surprising news. We shall make no attempt to depict the surprise of the home folk. The offer was too gladly accepted and was used at once in the repurchase of the old farm, and with characteristic honesty the few hundreds in excess of what was needed for this was given to Therese for her father's sake.

This was the beginning of solid wealth for John junior, for his parents rightly said the farm ought to be his. In this his brothers and sisters concurred, so the transfer papers were made out. He thought so well of the coal mining company that had been formed that he persuaded his father to loan him a few hundred dollars to buy stock. In less than two years it had paid for itself and more, but this was his last "speculation." He decided the business too fraught with anxieties.

The log house had gone the way of the earth,

but the added rooms in which the younger Rachel had taken such a pride were still, good, and after being remodeled would make a cheery "evening place" for the father and mother, and it was here we saw them at the reopening of this story. In the course of time John had built his own great roomy house by the side of these, indeed connected by a door, and here at the reopening he lives with his wife and growing family of boys and girls.

A swift successor to Beauty carries him back and forth to his business, for the old mills, remodeled and rebuilt, have been his for many a day. A steady business man is he, recognized in the home church as one of its thorough-going, truest friends.

"Louise is coming home!" The news flew. All agreed in the wish of their mother that they should celebrate her coming by a family gathering. She would arrive about the first of May. Happy thought, why not celebrate the fiftieth anniversary of the wedding that occurred in Lynton in 'forty-three?

The broad acres of the old farm had never looked more beautiful than they did that bright May morning when the great farm house seemed literally alive with guests and children. Rose had not far to come; she was the wife of the prosperous farmer who owned the acres adjoining. Her own and her brother John's young people had been jealously watching the great orchard that for more than a week had been a snowy mass of bloom,

Grandmother had told of the old sweet wedding decorations and it had been their wish to reproduce them. Would the blossoms fade too soon? was the absorbing question. A row of Winter Greenings answered by delaying their bloom two whole weeks after the others, and when the anniversary dawned were radiant in their beauty. Great bowlfuls stood in every nook and corner, and Rose's eldest, a sweet lass of twelve named Rachel, capped the climax when she pinned a spray at her grandmother's breast, and arranged a smart modern boutonniere for her grandfather's lapel.

The Rev. Asbury and family had arrived. His hair is whitening rapidly. It is yet an interesting question in psychology whether or not one grows to be so affected by his profession or calling that it becomes in a sort of a way a kind of badge. At any rate you would have taken this man for a preacher anywhere, and a western one at that. Perhaps the unconventional style of his dress and demeanor suggested the latter, or it may have been his ready utterance and earnestness in regard to sins both private and national. There is not really a hint of conservatism in his whole make up.

God has been very gracious in his dealings with this our erstwhile young minister, and he has become a strong factor in both church and state. The word "state" is used advisedly, for during these last twenty years a great moral triumph has been won, and when the tocsin of war sounded he

and his brethren to a man girt on their swords of
ready argument, convincing logic, and prayer of
faith. They spoke while standing on goods boxes on
the open streets on week days, and within pulpits on
the Sabbath. Every school house became an orator's platform from which this new movement was
heralded. There could be but one result. To-day,
in all that state there is not a legalized place like
that in which Richard Newton received his death
wound.

Those were heroic days! The younger children,
even now, love to gather while Aunt Emma tells of
burning churches, of threatened lynchings, and
sometimes of blood shed.

Edward, the quiet scholar, the ready writer and
apt scientist, is also here. His "maiden article" was
followed by many others. To-day he is a valuable
contributor to many of the current periodicals.
Contrary to his mother's expectations, he too entered the ministry, but under circumstances very
different from those of his brother Asbury, for his
first charge was a city mission. He did most excellent service here for two years and it was here he
found his bride. She had grown up in a parsonage.
His ministerial prospects seemed unusually bright,
but just at this juncture his alma mater give him
an urgent call to teach in its halls, offering him
what he most loved, the Sciences. Finally he
yielded. It was as well, for time has proven him a
rare educator. To-day he is a recognized authority

upon botany. Go into your high school, and more than likely the authorized text book on that science will bear his name.

Ruth Warren and her husband, with their children, have come from the far West. For years he has been president of a western college that is taking front rank among its more pretentious eastern sister. It would take a great deal of time and space to tell the half of Ruth's life successes. She has been the companion, fellow student and inspiration of her husband. She is an intelligent factor in the church, and a sweet and gracious mother; in short her womanhood is but the fruitage of the promise of her girlhood.

But the centre of attraction to all, even to the elders as well as the younger ones, was a sweet-faced elderly woman with frost sprinkled hair, of whom at first the younger ones stood a little in awe. How could they think a missionary whom they had never seen a bit of common flesh and blood like themselves. But a few cheery laughs from the missionary and that vanished. And how proud they were of their own Aunt Louise, of whom each has heard all their lives. Is it true, or do we imagine it that sometimes her gaze rests most lovingly upon that other sweet young Louise Stevenson, the babe of twenty years ago, who has just completed the course at her "Uncle Earnest's college," or that with a peculiar fondness she caresses the soft white hand that lies in her lap. Perhaps, though, it is all our fancy, for she is the life of the gathering. What marvelous stories she tells of far away China, and of the mission life. It all sounds so grand that half the younger ones are secretly resolving to become missionaries.

We had not noticed that in this group there are two strange faces; not strange, either, for we have seen them before. One of them is sitting near Ruth Warren. It is the quiet, happy face of Therese, with the heartache all gone.

All of Ruth's written promises were fulfilled. After she and her husband had returned and he was settled in his work, he did interest himself in her behalf and secured for her a position as teacher. So it came about that she made her home with Ruth, as was suggested. Ruth greatly encouraged her to active Christian work, and in her heart grew up the peaceable fruits of righteousness, and the dreadful past slipped away. Finally when one of the best and most prosperous business men of the city asked the really handsome Mrs. Les Page to share his name and home, she consented. There was little romantic fervor about this second marriage, but Therese was as well satisfied. Since that day her life has been a constant joy, and a happy circle of boys and girls is growing up around her hearthstone.

That remarkably handsome lad over there, who with a careless grace has just thrown his arm about Aunt Louise, somewhat to the discomfiture of the latter's own neices and nephews is Therese's eldest. She calls him Richard.

Marie, too, is here to honor the day. She and her daughters are resplendent in elegant clothes. She is quite as dainty and pretty as ever. Her husband is a careful business man, and there is no reason to think that life will ever be otherwise than what it is, a succession of luxuries, but she feels strangely out of place among those to whom, though neat and well dressed, clothes are only a necessary adjunct, and whose conversation runs entirely upon questions and topics of which she has scarcely heard.

Poor Marie; she has lived and is living her narrow little life. The prevailing styles and petty local society triumphs have been her horizon. She reads a little of the daily papers, especially that part which describes society's doings, indulges in a novel occasionally, but of the great world of thought and of the day's moral battles she is ignorant. Pity for poor Marie and her kind.

Her daughters have neither her beauty nor her dainty ways. Indeed, as we catch the startling slang that falls from their lips we fear they border on rudeness. Margaret, the eldest, is older than Asbury's Louise. She is already a blase young lady who has quaffed every cup of pleasure society has to offer. She with her younger sisters finds this gathering very "stupid," although the young folks have planned bicycle races up and down the shady, gravelled lane, and are performing miracles of grace with Indian clubs and dumb bells, and have even after a great deal of trouble, erected a tennis court in the grassy meadow beyond. "But such things are so childish."

We have spent so much time in noting the guests we can hardly look in at the groaning table, nor pause to offer our congratulations and well wishes to the aged pair whose hearts are so happy to-day. Nor can we stop to listen to the fun of the younger ones, nor even study the characteristics of any this younger generation, except to say that all bear the imprint of health. The mother of each set of children, whether in college town, Kansas parsonage, or of the free life of the farm, has made physical culture a specialty. Their clothes are made for a purpose, rather than for an end. Though one or two of the group have reached and passed the twentieth year, yet the talk is still of study, so we infer they are all walking closely in the paths of their elders. But the day is waning, Marie has gone to her home, Therese and her children have accompanied them.

The brothers and sisters gather in the dusk in the great parlors, and much of the family history is recounted. Reminiscence follows reminiscence, and it is not strange that often the hearty laugh rings out. But the reflections are not all thus cheerful, for that other happy couple who began life also fifty years before is remembered, and all grow hushed in genuine pity as the name is mentioned. Nor can much be said, for that sorrow lies too close to the heart of one of their own.

This aged couple has indeed reason for thanksgiving. As their children gather about them each comes as a servant of the King, and what matters it whether the world ever bestows its plaudits, the consciousness of an honest, upright life is sufficient reward.

> "To have acted well our little part,
> There all the honor lies."

*   *   *   *   *

In the dusk of that same evening a solitary figure, that of a woman, might have been seen picking her way among the older graves of the city cemetery. Presently she paused beside a sunken one, and leaning upon the plain shaft which marked it, she murmured the one word, "Richard!"

During this day of rejoicing brave Louise Stevenson had gone about with such an ache tugging at her heart, as her family little guessed.

When the tall and well formed lads and lasses had gathered about her and begged for a song, or the younger ones with greater freedom had clambered upon her knee, she had realized anew the depth of her loss, in that woman's richest crown of wifehood and motherhood had been denied her. Further it had been borne in upon her that she was a stranger in her own land, and though her family held her dear, yet they had learned to do without her. She had lost her place among them; plainly her "niche" was no longer here, but across the sea.

In a short time she must turn her face eastward; a few more years of work, and then her body would rest, not here as might have been its right, but there in a mission "God's Acre." Abandoning herself to her grief, she knelt by the grave of her youthful lover. The past came back so plainly. How beautiful he had been; how generous; how warm the impulses of his heart; how gifted; to what heights might he have climbed. But kneeling there as with lightning flash she saw the fatal web that had been woven about him from his very boyhood. She heard again the mazy tread of the home dance, caught the sparkle of the home wines, and listened to the cynical sneer concerning things holy.

She beheld the web tighten as the temptations of college life assailed him, and recalled the proud boast of his chosen college, that it was "broad, liberal, and unhampered by the narrowness of creed."

"My Darling Richard!" she moaned in her agony. "It is indeed true, men cannot gather grapes from planted thistles, and your wrecked life was after all but natural fruitage."

But alas, that the harvest should be so bitter!

THE END.

www.ingramcontent.com/pod-product-compliance
Lightning Source LLC
Chambersburg PA
CBHW020337030726
47496CB00007B/1925